When Your Standards
Are Compromised

When Your Standards
Are Compromised

Demona Elzey

TATE PUBLISHING
AND ENTERPRISES, LLC

Scripture quotations marked (KJV) are taken from the *Holy Bible, King James Version*, Cambridge, 1769. Used by permission. All rights reserved.

Scripture quotations marked (NKJV) are taken from the *New King James Version*. Copyright © 1982 by Thomas Nelson, Inc. Used by permission. All rights reserved.

This book is designed to provide accurate and authoritative information with regard to the subject matter covered. This information is given with the understanding that neither the author nor Tate Publishing, LLC is engaged in rendering legal, professional advice. Since the details of your situation are fact dependent, you should additionally seek the services of a competent professional.

The opinions expressed by the author are not necessarily those of Tate Publishing, LLC.

Published by Tate Publishing & Enterprises, LLC
127 E. Trade Center Terrace | Mustang, Oklahoma 73064 USA
1.888.361.9473 | www.tatepublishing.com

Tate Publishing is committed to excellence in the publishing industry. The company reflects the philosophy established by the founders, based on Psalm 68:11,
"The Lord gave the word and great was the company of those who published it."

Published in the United States of America

ISBN: 978-1-62147-846-1
1. Fiction / Christian / Short Stories
2. Religion / Christian Life / Inspirational
12.12.19

Table of Contents

Introduction

One's temperament can never be hidden from mankind. It cannot be trapped in the depths of one's soul, empowered by the objective in keeping it surreptitious. The true nature of the beast always reveals itself. An act of an event can be capable of disclosing one's concealed temperament. There are cases that the source of revenue or even a privileged position can alter one's behavioral makeup. They are moved by worldly possessions and positions, allowing themselves to be ruled and enslaved by it. This would compromise one's standards in being consistently surrounded by unconstructive influence.

In the case of this storyline in this book, one of the characters in the story was motivated in shifting his behavioral makeup. His new position of employment misrepresented him by the resources that were provided to him. The fame, money, women, and special privileges corrupted him, and his standards were compromised. It is easy to be enthused by a promotion in life. Many people want to enhance their way of living so their struggles would dissipate, but nothing in this world should change one's standards. Of course, there is an exception to the rule when an individual is lost in the world and is motivated in many ways to alter his or her lifestyle into the Lord's. The two women in the story had the eagerness in demeaning their standards by their desires of achievement. The lust in making a name for themselves decreased their value as women. Their mission, their drive, and persistence had them on a dark path of humiliation. One should implant themselves on a solid foundation and refuse to be moved by current or approaching circumstance.

If one is not able to recognize themselves when they look in the mirror, it's time to make that change.

This segment of the book, *When Your Standards Are Compromised*, has a different twist from my first book, *Soaring above Satan, Soaring above Self*. The book talks about one's character that has been compromised by their inner desires. The taste of what has been lusted over has left them weak and vulnerable. The characters in the story had gone too far but found themselves on the journey into God's open arms. In this book you'll find three fictional stories with the zest of God's Word. Through their secular method of living, they have found the goodness of God. From one catastrophe to the next, their afflictions had elevated for the depth in where it all began. On the map of God's design, He made away to have someone in place to expose Christ to them. With their newfound faith, they were able to harmonize during the state of their affairs, which makes God the baddest man in town.

Faith insinuates assurance, confidence, and trust. "Faith is the substance of things hoped for, the evidence of things not seen" (Hebrews 11:1). God is asking for faith of the size of a mustard seed. Now for those who don't know the magnitude of a mustard seed, let me tell you that it is very small. As for the three individuals who are in the storyline, faith has brought them through, and it is faith that will keep them. The Holy Bible has provided us examples that will give substance of the meaning of the word *faith*. It is faith that provides stability in our Christian walk. "For we walk by faith and not by sight" (2 Corinthians 5:7).

It is "by faith we understand that the worlds were framed by the Word of God so that the things which are seen were not made of things which are visible.

By faith, Abel offered to God a more excellent sacrifice than Cain, through which he obtained witness that he was righteous, God testifying of his gifts, and through it he being dead, still speaks.

By faith, Enoch was taken away so that he did not see death "and was not found, because God had taken him"; for before he was taken, he had this testimony that he pleased God.

By faith, Noah, being divinely warned of things not yet seen, moved with godly fears, prepared an ark for the saving of his household, by which he condemned the world and became heir of the righteousness which is according to faith.

By faith, Abraham obeyed when he was called to go out to the place which he would receive as an inheritance. And he went out, not knowing where he was going. By faith he dwelt in the land of promise as in a foreign country, dwelling in tents with Isaac and Jacob, the heirs with him of the same promise, for he waited for the city which has foundations, whose builder and maker is God.

By faith, Sarah herself also received strength to conceive seed, and she bore a child when she was past the age, because she judged Him faithful who had promised.

By faith, Abraham, when he was tested, offered up Isaac, and he who had received the promises offered up his only begotten son…

And it was by faith that Shadrach, Meshach, and Abednego displayed faith of the power of God when it was decided not to eat at the king's table and utterly refused to bow to the feet of the image of the king. It was then that the men were sent to the fiery furnace carrying the faith in God.

> Then the King Nebuchadnezzar was astonished; and he rose in haste and spoke, saying to his counselors, "Did we not cast three men bound into the midst of the fire?" They answered and said to the king, "True, O king." "Look!" he answered, "I see four men loose, walking in the midst of the fire; and they are not hurt, and the form of the fourth is like the Son of God."
>
> Daniel 3:24-25 (NKJV)

"But without faith it is impossible to please Him, for he who comes to God must believe that He is, and that is a rewarder of those who diligently seek Him" (Hebrews 11:3-5, 7-11, 6, 17, NKJV).

When all things failed and there was no one else to call upon, it was Christ that was considered. Even though God was the last for them to call upon, they carried the faith like no other to carry them out of their despair. Faith is the key to open many doors. I hope that you'll receive many blessings from teaching three short stories.

Too Cute

Welcome to the world of an individual who believes that she is too cute to worship God. Bend down on her knees and pray? Yeah right. She had everything that she possibly needed: married men. All the fine brothers were hitched. As long as they're rich and don't mind pleasing the sista, she didn't need God. Dodging the wives of her lovers was a way of life. Her girlfriends used to play the same playa games but discovered God for themselves and built an enriched life. Sasha Green, on the other hand, had a different perspective in life. Sleeping in married men's beds, getting treated in the finest restaurants, jewelry, fine hotels—the girl was livin'. With her cheating and pleasing herself in living the good life, she left a trail of broken homes. It was during her man hunting that she found the man of her dreams. The man was loaded and single. With her eyes fastened to her prize, she took a step closer, but little did she know that she was stepping into a trap.

God, Sasha Green will soon know the Word. God will become the man of her dreams.

I swung my hair back, looking fly, wearing my pumps high to the sky; my skirt so tight you can see the crease of my thighs; my shirt so low so my pups can run wild. I'm too sexy to be approached. I'm too hot to feel your touch, so betta step aside, clicking my heels and puppies jumpin'. I need a man to jump this ride, but people keep telling me I need the Word of God. I pushed my hands up, viewing my manicure. I didn't want to hear that God could be a cure, vaporizin' my sin to the sun. I'm too cute to worship God. Why are you looking at me so strange? I know I'm lookin' cute. You're just mad that you cannot get this. Look, buster, I'm not a hooker. This sista has a part-time job and needs a brotha with a truckload of money because I'm sick of being underprivileged. You see, my friends used to feel me, getting on a road of the easy life. But my sista girls found God and left my side. That's okay. I'll just work on my stride because I'm too cute to worship God. You have to see that I love living a fast life. Can you see that I like living a good life? I've been in fancy homes, sleeping in king size beds, dodging the husbands' wives like a football player. I didn't have money to go to school. I had good parents, but they were poorer than the value of a penny. They did everything they could, but I need a man so I can travel high in the society.

I'm searching for a good life. What can God do? I don't need God but a brotha who's meeting me at the Romano Café at 12:30 p.m. Yeah, that is what I'm talking about. Looking in through the window of Romano Café, watching my prize through these sore eyes. A piece of work, I have to say. He has no shame in looking good. Let me get in there and start to play. Who knows, this might be my future to be the queen I always wanted to be. He rose to my approach. A gentleman I see. We talked about me, and we talked about him; the conversation was like magic. Who needs Walt Disney when the magic is here? A single man in his early thirties. Ah, I had to pinch myself because this cannot be real. I wondered, *What's the catch?* as the magic grew through lunch and dessert. With his glass of wine held up high, he smiled and said he had a good time. I was careful to not to use my street slang. I didn't want to scare the brotha but to hook up with my future lova. Lunch was divine—I just picked that word up. I have to keep my eyes on this brotha; he's a trophy I didn't want to lose. He helped me with my chair, checking me out. We walked out of the restaurant laughing and smiling at one another. We faced each other in front of the restaurant, and it was then he reached over with his chocolate brownie lips and kissed my cheek. A gentleman I see. With his phone number in my bra, my puppies are tamed, keeping my treasure hidden inside. I worked my stride, feelin' that he's watchin' from behind. I want to do this right because this sista is tired in being unhooked.

I met this brotha, Joseph Reed, at an upscale dance club called the Y in Chicago. I made sure that I was dressed right and on my best behavior; everything else that night was a fairy tale. Well, no time to reminisce—I've learned that word too—but it's time to go to work.

I work part time in Macy's skincare department, which means, in my case, "all ova." Anything that has to do with skincare—face, eyes, lips, hands, nails, and body—I'm there. I make a decent living with thirty-five hours a week at fifteen dollars an hour. I'm expectin' a raise in a week—a whole dolla, yeah.

Six hours have passed, and all the hell raisers passed my way. Can you see why I need a better life? I can travel when I want. I can go to spas to ease my stress, and I will have a man to caress my day away. May I say more? God is not needed for anything in my life.

13

Months had passed, and my relationship with Joseph still felt fresh and brand new. Each date was like the first—magic. I've attended school to get my AA degree. Have you noticed? I've been talking intelligently. One semester down, and the others are almost completed. One more year and I'm done. Joseph was paying for everything, so I will continue to get As and Bs. With my academics, I don't know what is next in line, but I know I have a lova who is pleasin' his suga.

In two weeks and four days exactly from my final exams will be our one-year anniversary as a couple. When I look at him now, I don't see or think about money as much. I can't believe it; I think I'm in love. I can't believe that I'm getting everything I wanted. My sistah girls missed out on this fortune for their misfortune. I have a great man that is swimming in money, and to top it all off, I'm in love. I need God? God who? God what? I'm sittin' on top of the world, lookin' too cute to get these precious knees dirty to worship some God I have never seen. I love my sistah girls, don't get me wrong. They have found their good husbands wrapped around in a great family atmosphere and great careers, but it didn't come easy. I'm a sista who doesn't want to sweat in getting her life off the ground, please. As long as I'm pleasing my man in becoming more intelligent, that will be all I need. He pays for almost everything, so I don't have to do much. An easy life, you see. I don't want to get my hands too dirty when I have a man to keep them clean, do you feel me?

Well, finals came and gone, I'm feelin' victory in my game. A week and three days are left, and I can't wait to spend it with my man. I gazed at the diamond ring, sparkling to my eyes, watching him slipping it on my finga. I hope my dreams come true. Well, in a week and three days, I need to do something to keep my mind off this.

It has been a while since I communicated with my girlfriends. Is it possible that they are still talking to me? I went home in my day of victory. I have no exams or nights of studying. I am a free sistah. Work will be looking for me tomorrow.

The day is still young, time to play. I sat down on my cozy chair with my legs crossed, trying to generate enough energy to call my sistah girls. One ring lead to another and another, but when I was about to leave a message, I heard a *hello*. I said it was her girl Sasha, but in her voice, she was glad I was still alive. I told her my plans, but she had one of her own. Her and her husband had play date planned, and my second sistah friend was on vacation. Well, work was sounding good—too good.

The next day, work was the same, and the customers never disappointed me with their bad attitudes. Work kept me so busy I almost forgot my one-year anniversary. Bling-bling, bring the ring here. I haven't heard from my man in a week. Business trips are like a plague; it is infecting our time togetha.

My manager walked up when I was about to leave for the day. He handed me an envelope and walked away. Okay, hello to you. I opened the envelope, and it was an invitation from my man to meet him at the Romano Café, where we had our first date. Wow, a gentleman I see. Walking down the street with my heels clickin' and my puppies tamed, boy, has this sistah changed. Looking through the window of the Romano Café, I was viewing my prize through these sore eyes. I can't wait for my bling-bling to find its way on my finga. Once again, he rose to my approach; it was like déjà vu. We lip-locked, which felt like eternity; I knew this day was the day. We sat down, and he asked how my day was. The same'o, same'o I told him, but I didn't go into details. I thought, *Hey, where is my* happy anniversary, *honey? I miss you. I love you. Will you marry me?* But instead he asked me how my day was! He leaned back into his chair, grabbed a dozen of red roses next to his chair, leaned toward me, and said "Happy anniversary." *No! Were my thoughts spoken aloud? Did he hear me?* With my thoughts runnin' wild, I almost forgot to say *thank you* and *happy anniversary.*

Our dinnertime together was perfect, but no ring. I've been putting out, and no ring. I shouldn't complain. My chocolate lova is still taking care of his brown suga.

After dinner, Joseph wanted to take me to a coffee shop/restaurant. His college bud owned it, and he thought it would be nice for dessert. The place was called the Landmark Grill and Lounge. It was breathtaking. Should this sistah get her hopes up or chill on the thrill in getting her ring? Well, let's see where this journey will take me.

Hand in hand, Joseph escorted me to meet his friend, and shortly after, his friend escorted us to a table.

"Your friend is nice," I told Joseph, but he didn't hear me. I could see in his face that something was on his mind—a ring perhaps. I was going to say something, but I remained quiet.

I placed my hands in his, and magically he came back to himself again. He looked at me and smiled. One of the waiters came to the table to take our order and gave us a bottle of champagne on the house. After that I knew tonight was the night of my proposal. Joseph took my hand since there was no room to get down on his knees and proposed. Of course, I said *yes*. Bling-bling, the ring has finally found its way on my finga. My eyes lit up like a Christmas tree. I didn't want to examine the ring in front of him, so I'll wait until tonight. I have all night to have all my lights turned off so my ring can bling-bling in the dark. He has money and kindness. Did I fall onto the lap of the man of my dreams? I couldn't help but to embrace him. Boy, did that word come in handy.

With champagne, we had the grape-apple pie caramelized, with caramelized grape-apples, caramel sauce, and caramel ice cream. We shared, of course. The idea of eating this dessert by myself would blow me up and out of proportion. All evening, I was walking on air. In Joseph's SUV, I was floating above my seat. When driving me back home, there were only a few words spoken. We smiled our way to my apartment, and it was good enough for me. He didn't stay with me that night; he said he had an early riser. That was okay with me; I was planning to turn all my lights off and watch my bling-bling shine on my finga.

The next day, I called my girl and told her I was getting married. I heard a large sound and knew she dropped the phone. She wanted to know if he was planning to leave his wife, and I told her he was not married. Then she wanted to know if he was legit, and I said yes. I explained to her that he owned a successful art gallery and life was treating him very well. She was happy for me, but I could also sense that she was skeptical about my man. I didn't care. She needed to get over it because I was getting married.

It wasn't long that Joseph wanted to get together to make plans for the wedding. I couldn't believe it. He wanted to plan for the wedding. I was thinking about a large wedding, but he was talking about a small one. He wanted to get married at the courthouse. He said that he didn't have any family members and didn't find it necessary to have wedding in an empty church. Who was I to complain? My parents died some time ago; the only people I had in my life were my girlfriends. I told him that I wanted my girlfriends to attend the wedding, and he said okay. So a date was set for two months. I needed to call my girl to let her know.

Everything was moving so fast, and I wanted to slow down a little. It was nothing for me to do but chill. So I called my girlfriend Denesha and told her to sit down because she would not believe it. I told her that I was getting married in two months. Again, she was happy for me, but she was still skeptical. Samantha, my other girlfriend, just got back from her vacation yesterday, and Denesha filled her in on everything that was going on. Samantha told Denesha that she would not support me in anything that I was doing until

I gave my life to God. I got off the phone with Denesha and called Samantha. Samantha's husband picked up, said his greetings, and handed that phone to Samantha. We talked for a while; she explained that she didn't want to support something that wasn't right. She claimed that she was my girl but didn't accept how I was living my life. When I hung up the phone with her, I wasn't mad. I knew she was jealous that I was marrying a rich man, but who can blame her? He's my man, not hers. Anyway, time to move on. I have a wedding in two months.

There was a lot to do and very little time to do it. I only had a month to go, and I still had to sell some of my furniture. The manager of the apartment complex allowed me to get out of my contract with him early. He was proud of me in getting my life on the right track. I didn't know people were watchin' me. Samantha was still on my mind. I felt sorry for her in thinking that I needed God in my life. If she only knew that my life has been pretty good without God in it. That's okay, though; this sistah was on her own. I have moved most of my things to Joseph's place and was still working on getting the big things out of the way. Salvation Army was sounding good—real good. Well, it was time to rest this brown suga because her chocolate lova was waiting for her to pick out a dress. Shortly after meeting my man at Macy's, we found a dress for his sore eyes. We had lunch and went back to his place. I don't need to explain what had happen next.

The time has arrived. I didn't see my girlfriend until the day of my wedding. At the courthouse, Denesha was alone. There was no husband or kids. What's up with that? I have to claim down, woosaw sistah girl, woosaw. Who cares who comes and who stayed home; this sistah girl is getting married.

My experience at the courthouse was unusual. The judge himself was acting strange. He was constantly looking at the door to see if someone was coming. There was only a little time to talk with my girl. She was glad this day was coming and hugged me and to say congratulations.

Everything was startin', and I was gettin' very nervous. The judge was standing in front his desk, and Joseph and I were standing in front of him. My girlfriend was standing behind me, and a security guard was standing in front of the door. I thought it was strange, but hey, I was getting married.

The ceremony was short and intimate. I could have played this ceremony ova and ova in my mind because the words that were exchanged were unforgettable. We were off to our honeymoon. I waved to my sistah girl before the limo drove off. Huh, what can I say?

You can now call me Mrs. Sasha Reed, the queen of Chicago. For a couple of weeks, we spent our honeymoon in Hawaii. The honeymoon kept the bed rockin'. I was on cloud nine, and please don't make me fall. For all I care, this dream could last foreva.

On the way back home, I was confused. The ride was nice, but the ride home was not the direction we needed to take. We were traveling outside of Chicago. South Barrington, Illinois, was where we were going. The limo dropped us off at 221 Wood Oaks Lane. I had to get out of the limo to see the whole house. Joseph explained the house was 4,920 square feet when he was touring me around the dual-turned staircase home. The house had five bedrooms, four bathrooms, a study, a first and second floor, sunroom, gourmet kitchen, four-car garage, and a luxurious whirlpool hot tub. Did I mention that I was the new queen of Chicago, well, South Barrington? The house was already furnished with Joseph and my things combined. Boy, a big diamond ring, a husband, and now a castle? Look out, queens of the universe. With a ribbon and bow wrapped across my chest, I couldn't wait to give my new husband his gift to unwrap, besides, with our new master bedroom why wait.

After our first year of marriage, I was still on cloud nine. Joseph wanted me to stop working, and I wasn't saying much on that idea. He said he didn't want his wife working since he was making plenty to take care of things. We had a house-cleaning service that came by the house three times a week, and that is all. When it came to food, he didn't want anyone to cook his food expect for himself and his wife. Did I say that I was still on cloud nine? With my new Lexus LS 460 car, I was able to get around. I visit my sistah girls from time to time, but the distance between us had kept us from seeing each other on a frequent basis.

School was ova and done with, and I was bored. Joseph was on countless business trips, and I only attended half of them. I'm not complaining. When he misses me, I get the bling, baby. I go shoppin' and volunteer at the shelter in Chicago. I ran into some friends along the way, and they hated me for where I am. Please, don't hate a sistah because of the bling.

For the next two years, life was fabulous. We had Christmas parties at the house and parties throughout the year. Joseph and I would set up his mini art gallery at our home for people to privately buy whateva they liked. Yeah, life was good. One night, life wasn't treating me the way it should. I woke up in the middle of the night throwing up and feeling nauseated. I couldn't get rid of this headache and was feeling too tired.

One day during my doctor's visit, I explained to the doctor that I was not feeling so hot. I explained my symptoms, and he sent me to the lab to give urine and a blood sample. I hope I wasn't coming down with the flu or something. I went to the ATM to get some cash for groceries, but I wasn't able to get any money. I went inside to see why I wasn't able to get money out of my bank account. I couldn't believe my ears when I found out that my account was frozen. I couldn't do anything about it. I called Joseph to see what was going on. He didn't tell me much but just said, "I'll see you at home."

Around seven o'clock at night, my husband came walking in the door. I couldn't start foaming at the mouth about our account being frozen, but instead he came up to me and embraced me and said that he called the bank and corrected the problem. After that night, we didn't speak about it again. Joseph didn't want me to go anywhere until it was time to see the doctor again.

On the day of my doctor's appointment, Joseph escorted me to the doctor's office. He hugged me and kissed me passionately. Well, well, is this making up for not being around enough? I had a surprised look on my face, and he couldn't help but to kiss me again. He said he would pick me up after my office visit; I just needed to give him a call. Going into a small room to get my results was nerve-racking. Life was good, what now?

The doctor came in smiling. Boy, I didn't know that my misery was amusing. He closed the doctor, placed his hands in his pocket, and said, "You're pregnant."

My smile finally matched his, and I was on my way to call my husband. The doctor wanted me to make a follow-up appointment with him soon, but calling my husband was my first priority. I called Joseph up just to get his voice mail. A half an hour later, I couldn't reach him. I called home, his job, and his cell for an hour. I decided to get my pregnant butt home by catching a cab.

When I reached the house, I saw a "For Sale" sign on the lawn. When I placed my key in the keyhole, the door opened. Joseph wasn't himself. He told me to get in the house, and I asked him why he didn't answer my calls. He had my clothes in his hands and threw them at me; he told me to put them on. A pair of stretched jeans, a sweater, sneakers, and a coat was what I put on. I told him that I didn't like his attitude and that I was pregnant. He took a deep breath and threw me out of the house.

I looked at him with tears in my eyes. "Why are you doing this?"

He said that it didn't pay to play around with someone else's husband. I thought Joseph lost his mind. I didn't cheat on him. He explained that he has a sister named Cami, the person's husband I cheated with five years ago. He also explained that I was caught cheating with two other husbands whose wives he knew. He said I broke up the homes of all the husbands I cheated with. I was just looking for someone with money to take care of me, and I thought Joseph was the one. His final words were, "It's time to pay the piper." I yelled and screamed, asking him if our relationship, our marriage meant anything to him. He slammed the door, and there was only silence. I started to walk away from the house. Thoughts were roaming in my mind about spending three years with a man I thought I knew. He did all of this to get back at me. I stuck my hands in my pockets and found a handful of tissue in my left pocket and $800 cash in my right.

I caught a cab to Chicago, a place I was very familiar with. I called my girlfriend Denesha, but she wasn't home. I didn't know what to do. I was homeless, pregnant, and scared. I had no other choice but go to the shelter. My cloud-nine days were gone. A couple of women recognized me, pointing fingers and welcoming to their crew; there was nothing else to do. One of the shelter workers took me to a homeless shelter for mothers. The agreement from the homeless facility was to find a job within the six months' time period or I was placed out in the streets. Didn't they know I was pregnant? I had hit rock bottom and hard. I gave up in callin' Denesha and Samantha. I was too embarrassed. I told them that I didn't need God, and I still didn't. Look where I am now. I have nothing.

During the months of my pregnancy, I found a job room cleaning in a fancy hotel. Being around Joseph helped me with my speech and elegance. I worked hard for fourteen dollars an hour. On my days off, I had the incentive to travel down to the courthouse where Joseph and I were married and see if they could force Joseph to help me. I inquired about the judge who married us, and the woman said she never heard that name before. I said it has been two years, and she said she'd been there for eleven years. I stepped away from her and remembered seeing her that day. I explained to her that I was married down the hall and to right in where she was seating. I went as far as informing her that I was married next to suite 311. She was kind enough to allow me to escort her to a room where I was married. Up to this day, I couldn't believe that I led her to the break room. The room was the size of an office and perhaps even two. I apologized to the lady and went home. From the time we first met at the Y, everything was a set-up—fake judge, fake husband, I'll bet the friends were fake too. This sistah girl is not trippin'. I had a job, and now I needed to focus on my baby.

Room cleaning couldn't get any worse. I was six months along, and I was on my feet long hours. I was tired and missin' the good life. I worked until I was nine months pregnant and left on maternity leave. I had my baby boy two weeks later. It's a shame that I had no one there for me in my time of joy. I wanted so badly to call my sistahs, but I didn't need any frowns and their judgmental mouths.

Three months later, I went back to work. A trusting neighbor was kind enough to watch my child, Jeremiah. I went to work just to get fired. Since I was gone, they took the liberty to hire someone else. Did you know I raised hell? The police came when things started to heat up. They escorted me out and warned me to never step foot in this hotel again. Here I was, down on my luck. I was without a job and had a new baby to feed. For two months I looked for a job, and nothing. I didn't want to go on welfare and become a typical black person for everyone to talk about—the one who is considered lazy or the one who doesn't want to work. Therefore, I found myself on the streets with thirty dollars to spend. I had a crying baby on one arm and was wiping my tears with the other. All my fly days were gone. I looked at Jeremiah and told him he had the wrong mother. I didn't know what to do next. I couldn't walk these streets with my pups untamed just to find a man to win this prize. The only puppies that would be jumpin' were to feed my son.

In the winter nights, my son's crying echoed into my ears, and there wasn't anything I could do. He was so hot, and I knew he was running a fever. He cried so much he fell asleep, and I began to weep. I got on my precious knees and prayed to God. I didn't need instruction in how to pray, it just came out like I was withholding this moment for so long. I repented all my sins like Samantha told me to do. I asked the Lord to forgive me and that I wanted to be His child. I was crying so much the tears blinded my sight in seeing my sleeping child. I also cried until I fell asleep.

The next day I felt different—I felt relieved. When I opened my eyes, I was in the same place with my back against the wall. I gave God a *thank you* and took my child to a clinic. Two hours later, my son had seen a wonderful doctor. He gave what was needed for my son and asked me to stay so he could make a phone call. I didn't care. A warm building and my baby stopped crying.

Boy, what had happened to the doctor? Twenty minutes, brother, where are you?

I heard a knock on the door, and the person walked in. Samantha? Apparently the doctor told her my profile, but I discovered that the doctor was her husband. Samantha embraced me and wanted us to stay at the guesthouse a hundred feet from their home. I was paralyzed with shock. She shook me and repeated herself. Did God provide this for me? I took her proposal and traveled to my new home. I cleaned up, and Samantha bought some clothes for me and my son. I told her the whole story over coffee and pastries in her gourmet kitchen. Her lips didn't open with judgment; instead she came to where I was sitting and hugged me. Were we in the twilight zone? She welcomed me to God's family. She wanted me to stay as long as I wanted in order to get my life back on track.

I already had a babysitter, Samantha with her three young ones of her own. I was set in going back to school. Since I had already received my AA degree, I went straight to a four-year college and signed up for psychology. I wanted to help women and to teach them that they didn't need a man to travel high in society. I want to reveal to them that they needed God in their lives and to believe that they could make it in this world.

I watched my son grow up to a preschool age. It was hard letting go, but we were all growing up and moving on with our lives. I'd never been so close with my sistah girls. We had more things in common than our friendship. I'm still paying for what I've done, but I know God will help me through. He has shown me that He is greater than anything of this world.

I graduated with honors, and it felt good. I worked with counselors and psychologists for three years, and they supported me in opening my own practice. But wait and see how God works. You see, I was blessed with a resort area of my own. It was small, but it was mine. I was able to give my patients beautiful scenery with a waterfall, flowers, trees, and a gazebo. The building had many windows honoring women to view God's green earth. I've ministered to the women as well as helped them with their addictions in living a wealthy lifestyle. Life is good, but most of all God is good. I have traveled "through the valley of the shadow of death," but the Lord shined His love and guided me through (Psalm 23:4).

I will make sure my son will be raised in a loving church environment, exposing him to the goodness of God. I have changed and forgiven those who hurt me and those who cursed my existence. I wanted to find Joseph and apologize and to let him meet his son. As a new woman of God, it was only right to give Joseph a chance to gain a relationship with a son he never met.

I traveled high and low to find Joseph, but when the search was over, I made sure my four-year-old was with me. I walked up to him; he didn't know how to act. I was dressed in my professional clothing, knowing that I was looking and feeling good with my new life. Joseph began the conversation with a smart remark, asking me if a man dressed me up and was taking care of me. Before I lost focus in the real reason why I made the effort in searching for him, I exemplified that I came to apologize and to say that I had forgiven him. I continued on to say that he was one of the reasons why I got my life together. I gave him my business card with my license number on it in order for him to see that my practice was indeed legit.

Before I attempted to introduce father and son, Joseph was on his knees, introducing himself. I told Jeremiah that he was his father, but I knew it would take a while for Jeremiah to warm up to Joseph. Joseph hugged me, which took me by surprise, and said that he was proud. He apologized as well and asked to be forgiven. I thought, *Hey, if God can forgive me of my sins, who am I to say that I cannot do the same?* I forgave him, and a weight was lifted. He emphasized that he still loved me. He couldn't completely follow the plans his sister conjured up. He continued to say that he was searching for me the day after I was thrown out of my own home. When he couldn't find me and his unborn child, the guilt consumed him. He also fell on his knees to seek God for salvation. "I am a true Christian," he said. He had changed his life around. I had a warm feeling that he was telling the truth. We took our relationship slow. There was no fornication for this sistah.

My sistah girls thought I was crazy to generate a new relationship with him, but it felt right and genuine. The best thing was that God was the foundation of this relationship.

In a year and a half of dating, we were married in a crowded church. I couldn't be happier. For three years, our family grew, and our marriage was a God-based fairy tale. He didn't go on business trips like he had done before. Teleconference was the new thing now. We kept our relationship built on the foundation of God. People can change. But are you willing? I know I did. Not every story ends with a happily ever after, but having God in your life and meeting with Him in heaven is a happily ever after.

Wait now, there's more. You must remember God is the creator and the finisher of all things. There's a message in the Holy Bible that you should know the moral of this story, the teaching of His Word. Now let me enlighten you in what I've learned from this and what I want you to become skilled in.

Quoting from the *Spirit-Filled Life Bible* (KJV):

> Why do you boast in evil, O mighty man? The goodness of God endures continually. Your tongue devises destruction, like a sharp razor, working deceitfully.
>
> You love evil more than good, lying rather than speaking righteousness. Selah.
>
> You love all devouring words, you deceitful tongue.
>
> God shall likewise destroy you forever; He shall take you away, and pluck you out of your dwelling place, and uproot you from the land of the living. Selah
>
> The righteous also shall see and fear, and shall laugh at him, saying,

"Here is the man who did not make God his
strength, but trusted in the abundance of his riches,
and strengthened himself in his wickedness."
But I am like a green olive tree in the house of
God; I trust in the mercy of God forever and ever.
I will praise You forever, because You have done
it; and in the presence of Your saints I will wait on
Your name, or it is good.

Psalm 52:1-9

Did you see me in this passage? I was seeking all the riches
on this earth, and I was a willing participant in getting what
I wanted in any way I could. I was utilizing the tongue of
the wicked to get what I wanted, when I wanted it. I was
weak in every way, so I fell into pool of sin and dwelled
in it. The destruction of the Lord is nothing I wanted to
experience, and you shouldn't allow it to be your fate. God
is good, and I've learned the hard way to discover that. We're
not immune when one gives their lives to God; Satan will
always be standing on the sideline, waiting for that special
time to attack. You'll never go wrong with Christ. Is it time
to make that special connection with Him?

The fool has said in his heart, "There is no God."
They are corrupt, and have done abominable
iniquity; there is none who does good.
God looks down from heaven upon the children
of men, to see if there are any who understand, who
seek God.
Every one of them has turned aside; they have
together become corrupt; there is none who does
good, no, not one.

Have the workers of iniquity no knowledge,
who eat up my people as they eat bread, and do not
call upon God?

There they are in great fear where no fear
was, for God has scattered the bones of him who
encamps against you; you have put them to shame,
because God has despised them.

Psalm 53:1-5

Amazingly, the ones who proclaim that there isn't a God
are the very ones who would fall on their knees, asking
the Savior for mercy. I was corrupted under the spell of
Satan. I had a choice to look the other way, but my mind
and heart were captured by the temptation of my desires. I
was devoured by the darkness of sin, but God woke me up
by withdrawing everything that I've built up for myself. I
thanked Him up to this day from the time He had rescued
me. He is still rescuing me when I temporally fall flat on
my face. The Lord is a merciful God, but sometimes when
God has had enough, you won't want to be around for His
judgment. Give your life today and discover the true love
of God.

Satan, I'm Going to Tell

The thing we practice in this world that is not of God has to pass away as we make our path to proceed the right way. In the family of God, we are in the world, not of it. We are as aliens in this world and are not easily embraced, because as God's people, we are different. We don't share the daily sinful practices from those who deny the Word of God.

God's people are not perfect, but we have a God in heaven that can help to deliver His people in our time of need. We just have to call on Him. The world is infested with crime and selfish desires that are wrapped with death, but God offers life for His people—an eternal life. Truly accepting Him as your Lord and Savior is the first step in the walk with Christ. The door is open; the path of the Lord lies beneath your feet. At times your walk will be rough, so keep your eyes on what's important and allow God to guide your footsteps. Lean to God's understanding, and not of your own, because the answers you seek, He can reveal it with understanding. When you walk with God, some friends may vanish from where you stand, but don't be discouraged. Continue to walk with Him.

Don't allow anyone to distract you, dragging you where it all began, because God has a lot to offer than a world that doesn't care. Walk with God you will not be disappointed.

It's moments like these you reflect on where your life is taking you, moments that consist of one's spiritual objectives. Living in a high-velocity society, some of us are observing the destruction of the world right before our eyes. With the devastation of this world, one must contemplate if they are spiritually correct with Christ.

Satan has an audacious character about himself, and his works have hit the airwaves stronger than ever before. There have been reports of a killings over a parking spot and killings in our schools and reports of rape, physical and mental abuse, road rage, and other disturbing acts that are not of God. The wickedness of man has taken its toll for many of the citizens of this nation to say *enough*. We as saints of God have to share the same audacious behavior against the wicked that is piercing our nation. The love of God should be hitting the airwaves as well and affecting those as they hear and see it. We need to be that roaring lion of Christ, fighting back against what Satan has taken and destroyed. As children of God, we need to take responsibility in learning what needs to be learned in order to survive Satan's playpen. Each time we spend with the Holy Father, the level of the relationship will broaden. Christ has already shown His love for us on Calvary when He died for our sins, and He is showing the same love today with His mercy and grace. It is time for us to show the same commitment.

We should not waste time in rising to our feet with boldness in the Lord and with faith. We can overcome the obstacles of Satan's irritable behavior. You see, Satan doesn't like the idea of his prey gaining knowledge of him as a thief who comes to steal, kill, and destroy (John 10:10). The prince of darkness wants to stay in darkness and for us to be completely oblivious of his existence. The less we know about him, the more powerful he will become. Knowledge is power, and for us to overcome the power of Satan, we have to know what we're dealing with. Remember that Satan doesn't want his dirty secret aired out for the public to hear. Let's keep this in mind for the believers and the nonbelievers. Satan is real, and he will stop at nothing to get us into his family.

Most of us are creatures of habit, and Satan preys on those who can lure themselves into his hand. Of course, with a little help of a revengeful heart of Satan, bait is thrown out there for the citizens of our nation to feast on. If we are not careful, we will be caught up onto his web. Satan has the ability to tempt us, but we have a choice to accept that temptation or deny it. Life itself is not fair, so why would you think Satan cares any more than the people of this world? If you're not an alien of this world, then you're part of it. You have joined an unthinkable time in damnation.

Stop, think, and reflect on the actions you have taken. Stop, think, and reflect on the things you have said. Does a lustful heart, a hunger of greed salivating over power and possession please the heart of God? Would a reflection of your spirit repulse you with a glance or be appealing to you? When the spirit of God is manifested in a host of a Christian, the appearance of action doesn't replicate the behavior of the enemy.

My name is Michael Evans. A door was opened with endless opportunities, but as an unsaved individual, I fell into a black hole without notice. With the temptation of the things I never had, I was weak and fell into a trap. It was a Christian who crossed my path one day, and instead of brushing him off, I found myself drawn in to what he had to say. It was with his help that I'm saved today, and it was because of Christ that I'm able to share my story. I hope my story will inspire you all.

A black veil fell upon my face, and darkness enslaved me. I thought it was all over, but it was probably what my enemies wanted me to think. The more I struggled in the midst of darkness, laughter traveled all around me, which I took as an indicator to give up. Anxiety fell into my heart and into my soul. This wasn't a place I wanted to be. I was given truth one day, and now there was no way of returning in the days of ignorance. But it didn't always used to be this way.

I wasn't a Christian. I was an ordinary guy from Perth, Scotland whose parents taught me to respect others and myself. I didn't involve myself in smoking, drinking, or taking any drugs. I didn't sleep around like an uncontrollable dog in heat that sniffed behinds and giddied-up for the ride. I would only be intimate with a woman who I was very serious with. I think of myself a kind person who doesn't get into trouble. I've considered others before myself. I'm an average Joe of 5'11," white male, physically fit, with short black hair, blue eyes and a shadowed beard. I'm little on the rugged side, but the ladies never seemed to mind. It all began when the walk of fame was placed beneath my feet. Being an actor gave me access to worldly and ungodly things, but being fresh in the business, my desires wanted it all.

Five years ago, cloud nine in my life was born from myth to a reality. My journey began, and my old life was placed to rest. Before the business of acting, I took on a job as cook at Mel's Diner after being laid off from Cisco System as a hardware engineer. On the busiest day of the week, we were short staffed, and I took on an additional contractual obligation in waiting tables. While cooking and waiting on tables, I had noticed an older fellow taking interest in me. Believe me, it made me a little nervous. I didn't swing that way. When serving him coffee, he asked me, "Sir, what is your name?"

I hesitated as long as it wasn't conspicuous to him. It wasn't long until my name spilled from my lips. "Michael Evans."

He explained to me that he was looking for a particular person to play a role in a movie. I couldn't believe that my heart found its way to a regular rhythm. He wasn't looking for a date. He quickly slipped me his card and asked to call him if I was at all interested in his proposal. I slipped his card in my pocket and thanked him on my way back to the kitchen.

In the core of flipping burgers and chopping veggies, I contemplated on the proposal of this strange individual. For any habitual person, there wouldn't be any hesitation regarding his proposal. This guy would have left this diner with a remarkable *yes*. My dilemma had changed.

On my lunch break, I tried his number. A receptionist answered the phone and presented her and the company's name. I lost my nerve and deliberately hung up the phone.

I pondered on how this new career was going to have an effect in my life. I loved the notion of making more money and very quickly, but at what price?

After work, I've decided to give this Mr. Louis Bloomberg a visit. From Mel's Diner, Universal Studios was tremendously close. Off Highway 101, in my daring act of bravery, I found myself pulling into a parking spot at the Universal Studios. I combed through the limitations of the property's parking lot. I was wandering aimlessly and found myself parked in front of a tree. When I was distracted with an unprocessed thought or two, it was then I heard my name called.

"Mr. Evans, I'm so pleased to see you here."

"Mr. Bloomberg, this wasn't planned."

"I cannot believe that I'm still amazed with your Scottish accent. You remind me of Gerard Butler in the movie *Machine Gun Preacher*, and this is why I have chosen you in my movie as a contracted killer. You have the sexy, rugged type look, and accent to top everything off." With the tree now behind me, I stood there and observed this below-average guy rumbling at the mouth.

"If time is on your side today, I would like for you to join me to my office."

"Okay," I said. I thought, *Why not?* I've been with Mel's Diner for so long change was something I didn't think would happen. Because of change, I was clothed with fear.

"Mr. Evans—"

"Michael, please, Mr. Bloomberg."

"Very well, Michael, have a seat please." I sat down as he made his way around his desk. "Well now, Michael, have you considered my proposal? With your Scottish accent and good looks, you'll play a marvelous part of a contracted killer." He continued about my part in the movie and summarized the storyline.

I leaned back on my chair and thought, *not too bad of a story.* I agreed to play the role of the contracted killer. Mr. Bloomberg swung his hand out to congratulate me and then handed me a contract. This was when it all started.

On my first day of work, Louis Bloomberg presented himself to the cast as the creator of the movie. "Hello everyone, for those who don't know who I am, I'm Louis Bloomberg, the creator and producer of his movie. We have a lot of work ahead of us, so there's no time to sit and chat. I understand that my assistant was kind to distribute the copy of the manuscript, so let's get moving." I watched as this below average stocky guy pushed up his glasses and got to work. In six months' time, the plot of the movie was clear. It didn't know that creating the movie was hard work. I've noticed that the actress, who played as a victim, had had her eyes on me ever since we started this movie. Who would want to get involved with someone who was fresh meat in the acting business? It was a good thing that I didn't pursue my curiosity about this woman. A buddy of mine decided to celebrate the progress of the film. Low and behold, Maggie Jones was barricaded with men on every angle.

"Don't look too hard, comrades," the bartender said. "That is what you call a classic whore," the bartender continued, and by the looks of it, he was scorned her by beauty and charm. In the case of Maggie, she involved herself with the high-ballers. She would use them and lose them, which brought up the question that I couldn't answer: *Why would she concentrate on me?* As soon as the question was raised, I dismissed the thought. I glanced back at her on the way out the restaurant; she noticed my departure and smiled. My buddy Keith tugged at me, which brought me back into reality from my tempted thought. I escaped her web that day, but I knew it wasn't the end of her deception.

The day had finally come when the movie was released to the public. Over the weekend alone, the movie made over $252 million dollars. My career grew from that point. I was then involved in other movies, commercials, and was a guest on some of the night shows. Life was good. Change was once my deepest fear, but now it was my ticket to a wonderful life. I've gone from one party to another, celebrating my success in my career. I was on cloud nine. It has been said that when you are at your peak, something is bound to happen. In fact, I didn't know how true the dictum was. But life went on. I attended one of the parties everyone wished they could attend, and by the looks of it, I knew why. A three-story festivity blew me over the edge. This place was in such an exclusive area, finding the next home would cost you a fifteen-minute drive.

On the way to the door, I flipped up my collar to my jacket and allowed my precious good looks to work their way through the front door. A social gathering occupied the first level of the building, but it wasn't what I was looking for. I made my way to the second level; I wasn't quite interested in dining and observing art. On the way up to the final level, I felt the vibration from the music flowing through my fingertips by the touch of the doorknob. I opened the door to the entrance of the party. The livelihood of this festivity stimulated my body to dance. The word *fun* was on the menu, and I wasn't stopping at anything to order it.

At the bar, I had to sit down and replenish my body after dancing. From across the room, I visualized a work of art. She was chatting with Maggie until she noticed my interest. When I smiled at her, she propelled her way from Maggie. When Maggie grabbed her arm, her acquaintance pushed her off. I didn't know what that was about, but the only thing I knew was I didn't want Maggie anywhere around me. She glided her way to the bar.

"Hello Mr. Evans. I've noticed you watching me across the room. Do you like what you see?"

"Impressive, Miss…"

"Ms. Heisler. Claire Heisler." She extended her hand, waiting for me to give her mine. From the stool at the bar, she crossed her silky legs, giving me flash of what was to come. "So, Mr. Evans, tell me something I don't know about you."

I thought, *There we go with the Mr. Evans again.* "Michael."

"Okay, Michael. Are you here alone?" I knew she was fishing around to see if I had a girlfriend, but with her low- and short-cut dress and a body to bring the guys to their knees, I would have forgotten about my girlfriend if I had one.

"Yes, as a matter of fact, I am."

She raised herself from the barstool with a smile. Her eyes were fixated on mine, and she said, "Let's dance."

We danced until the party ended. I escorted Claire to her car. She leaned her body against the door of her Lexus LS 600hL.

"Do you want to come to my place?"

Like taking candy from a baby, I was tempted—very tempted—but I was drunk. I couldn't shake off the feeling that I saw Claire with Maggie. I made up my mind.

"Not tonight." I liked Claire, but I couldn't trust her.

She gave me a seductive kiss that night, and I knew she was giving me another chance. She licked her lips as she drove off into the night. I slid into my Cadillac Escalade and leaned my head back onto the headrest. I was too wasted to drive.

The next day, I awakened with the sun beaming on my face. It was a surprise that I was still in my car and in the same clothes after dreaming that I was sleeping in my bed.

The brightness of the sun was intense; I wasn't able to open my eyes without squinting. I shielded the sun with the palm of my left hand to look for my shades. Bending over to the front seat of the passenger side, I grabbed the shades from the mat of my car. Lifting my body back to the driver side, my head felt like it was about to explode from this hangover. My mission at this point was to get home to mix my Bloody Mary cure for hangovers. I will never forget that day when everything hurts.

Driving down Bel Air Road, I sighed with relief. I pulled into my 1.4-acre home and traveled straight into the kitchen. In a tall glass, I mixed my concoction: 2 oz. of vodka, 6 oz. of tomato juice, 4 tsp. of Worcestershire sauce, and 2-3 drops of tabasco sauce. I stirred up my concoction with a celery stick and downed it until there was nothing left to see. I was ready to crash on the closest thing that was soft and reminded me of a bed.

When I finally came to, I felt something heavy on my chest. At first I thought it was my my German shepherd, Kori. But when I opened my eyes, I was disturbed to find out that it was Claire with my chest between her legs. I sat up, and her chest was pressed against mine.

With a sexy smile and her low-cut blouse she said, "I've been waiting for you to wake up about a couple of hours." I was wondering how she got into my place. "Oh, if you are worrying how I got in, your gardener let me in."

Interesting, my gardener was on vacation until tomorrow. "What are you doing here, Claire?" I was losing interest in her by the minute.

"I thought we would pick up where we left off. I hope you don't mind my boldness."

Bold was right. I removed myself from beneath her and walked into the kitchen for a glass of water.

"I think I better leave."

"I don't mind you being here, Claire, but you cannot come in unannounced or whenever you feel like it." I was upset, and she knew that. She didn't hesitate to leave, and I didn't hesitate to stop her. I didn't know what had gotten into me that day, and I don't think I ever will. I grabbed her and carried her into my bedroom, and I don't think I have to tell you what happened next.

As I lay next to her, her beauty captivated me. She smiled, and her face glowed. Usually when you offer meat to a dog, it doesn't matter if the dog is deaf or blind, he'll find his way. Temptation was offered on a silver platter, and like that dog, I went to get it.

Waking up once again, Claire was gone. A note was left behind with a rose, which I could tell came from the garden. The note said: "Thank you. I had a good time. If you wish to meet again, you know where you can find me." Temptation occupied my time; it was a time I wished I could have back. I got up and cleaned up. It was early Thursday afternoon, and I was more than grateful in not having another gig. Well, not just yet.

I lounged around the house and watched television, which was something I didn't normally do. I decided to pick up the newspaper at my front door after walking over it that morning with my hangover. The mailman crossed my path when I bent down to pick up the newspaper. Mr. Jones, my mailman, whom I called "Jonesy," came closer to the house, getting ready to fork over the mail.

"Hello, Mr. Evans, here's your mail. I see you have something from Mr. Bloomberg. You're a hot commodity. I think you have another job."

"Thanks, Jonesy."

I just finished a movie a month ago, but how can I say no to Mr. Bloomberg who got me into the business in the first place? I went back to the house and opened the mail just to find another movie script. The title was *Reflection to Perfection*, a suspense thriller. I took the time and read the script. Mr. Bloomberg had another Emmy on his hands, and just like the previous work, I wanted to be a part of it.

I called up Mr. Bloomberg and left a message that I was interested in playing the character that was suggested for me. That evening, I went out to the club where I could find Claire and took her to dinner. You know one date led to another, and before anyone could know, our faces were placed on the magazine *Us Weekly*.

My fans were with us on every special occasion. My life was no longer my own. On one of our dates, my aficionados ran up to me like children running after an ice cream truck. I autographed books, T-shirts, diaries, arms, legs—you name it. Claire had already left when I concluded in signing autographs. What did she expect? I was a celebrity.

Claire called up one night to enlighten me that she had a job working with some guy in the acting business. She was so thrilled she couldn't stop screaming. This guy, Henry Kardon, wanted Claire to work with him in a bar scene in a movie. Apparently this guy liked her face when he discovered us on *Us Weekly*. I was happy for her. She was also invited without my presence to a "who knows who" party.

Ever since Claire had been invited in doing diminutive part in a movie, I rarely saw her. It had been four weeks, and Claire and I had a relationship that became an apparition. We had seen each other approximately one to two hours once in a blue moon. The time had come to converse with Claire to see if she was in or out of this relationship. I knew just the place where I could find her.

I went to the club to find Claire just to discover her consulting with Maggie. When I moved closer into the vicinity of their lair, they were whispering amongst each other, darting their eyes upon me. Was I suspicious about the whole thing? No. I knew what I was getting myself into, but I was hoping that Claire would have been different. I pursed in worldly happiness, the women, money, and the acceptance from my aficionados that was my high. Claire, on the other hand, could fall into the cracks for all I cared. There were numerous fish in the sea, and I was the bait.

When I finally approached Claire, Maggie gave me the stare and took a hike. "Well, if it isn't Michael," Claire said, placing a fresh cigarette on the side of her lips. She didn't seem at all interested in me being there. "Oh, I failed to tell you that I don't need you anymore." She placed her hand on my chest and patted it with her devious stare as she turned to walk away.

"Whatever," I told her with no interest in her response. It was official on that day. Claire and I were a thing of the past, and in some way, I was relieved.

It was the following week when I had another woman hanging on my right arm going to the concert. The money was passed, cameras were flashed, and my new friend didn't know how to act. She once told me that she needed a break from her current relationship. As breathtaking as she was, I was content that she chose me as a candidate. The concert was rockin' that night, and it carried on into my bedroom at the hotel nearby.

When the next day came around, we got dressed and ordered room service. Well, what happened next I thought only happened in the movies. There was a knock that vibrated the door. I opened it, thinking it was room service, but I was serviced with a fist across my cheekbone. From opening the door to finding myself flat out on the floor, I raised up into a sitting position trying to get a clear view in who ram shacked me. From where I was sitting, I could only see the back of his head. Their confrontation made its way down the hall as the door of my hotel room remained ajar. I managed to stand on my feet.

"What's going on here?" I said, confused and now irritated with my new face job.

This guy turned around to face me, which gave me the opportunity to get a clear look. Well, I got a clear look all right; this guy had to have been six feet two inches, heavily built, with tattoos on one side of his neck, which probably ran down his arm if it was covered my fitted long sleeve shirt. "You're messing around with my wife."

I thought, *Wow, that was his wife?* I knew she was connected, but not married. Before I could explain, he created a new face job for me.

On the floor once again, I explained, "I didn't know she was married. I showed her a good time, and here we are." Now why did I say that?

"You get your own woman to f*** with and leave mine alone! You actors think that since you have a lot of money you can do anything you want without consequences! Well, you got your consequence. If I see you again around my wife, I'll do the world a favor and send you to your grave!"

He grabbed her left arm as she was reaching for her purse on the bed. I got up ready to defend her, but she looked at me and shook her head, telling me *no.* The husband darted his eyes at me on the way out the door. I backed away with my hands held up. I also noticed my nosey neighbors scattered around in the hallway to collect some juicy gossip to soak in. I closed the door immediately and sat on the edge of the bed. I leaned back and pondered about any possible way to have fun. Hitting the clubs was still the thing to remember. I got what I wanted, and the women kept me happy. But I was bored and in the search of something new. There was something missing in my life, and I needed to find it. It was time to get in touch with my friend Frank and get my feet wet in drag racing once again.

With the crowd cheering and the adrenaline pumping, it was another way to get the ladies and make some money on the side. Being a celebrity definitely had its advantages. I called Frank up and asked him to include me in a race. Frank talked about me so badly I wanted to change my mind about racing. I realized that I hadn't spoken to him over a year. After his two cents were placed, Frank asked for me to come to their hideaway on Saturday. It was about 2 1/2 years ago that I was involved in one of the drag races of the century. All the top dogs were there, and they were firing up their engines, getting ready to ride to keep their title. For some of us, we were out of their league. During the race, one of the amateurs lost control of his car and killed himself and two of the other drivers. Drag racing was never the same until now, but Frank still moved from one location to another, keeping the cops wondering.

It was two days away for the race, and I had to prepare. I had my 1971 Plymouth GTX. I didn't have to race, but I made sure that my ride was always ready for any challenge. With the Hemi engine, my GTX was going to give me a ride of a lifetime and the crown.

It was the night of the race. I got there early to get reacquainted with Frank. We talked almost an hour. His sister Marianna interrupted us to begin the race.

Frank raced to the door, "See you outside, Michael."

Marianna walked with me to my GTX. We were old friends from high school to community college. I'd received my AA degree, and she transferred to a university. People thought we were a couple, but I'd never considered in making it official. We lost touch when she traveled off to a university in Davis, California. It wasn't long for the spark of our friendship to sprout and blossom again. I guess I still had that charm.

I was now suited up for the race with engines roaring and my adrenaline pumping.

Marianna leaned over and said, "See you at the finish line."

She put a smile on my face, and I wanted so much to be the first person at the finish line. Frank gave the instructions, and the bullet was released from the chamber of his gun. The race had begun. During the race, I noticed that I had underestimated my opponents, but I was a natural-born dragster thanks to Frank. I couldn't be the baby in a cradle in losing this race. Frank would never let me live that down.

The finish was near, and the gal in the Nissan Skyline GT-R was making her way for the kill. The supercharger was in effect along with my secret weapon. As scheduled, Marianna was the first to see my face at the finish line. My winnings were given to Frank and Marianna, even though their refusal was made clear. It's not like I needed the money. I traveled back to their garage to celebrate.

"I'm glad you didn't embarrass me out there, Michael," Frank said.

We poured out a glass of scotch in jelly jars, raised them, and made a toast. We shot the breeze until Frank interrupted to announce that his little brother, Josiah, was getting married. I thought, *Man, Josiah is getting married.*

Josiah was a kid in middle school when Marianna and I graduated from high school. Boy, had time passed.

It was getting late, and it was time to depart this friendship reunion.

"You're going to join Frank at the bachelor party tomorrow night," Marianna said, targeting me for a *yes* response.

I couldn't say no, so I said, "I'll be there."

Frank, the oldest of us all, came up and grabbed me and gave me a hug. "It was good to see you. See ya tomorrow, kid." Frank had never been emotional, which brought me to the conclusion that something was wrong.

The next day, I combed through the city of Los Angeles to find a gift for Josiah. Too many years passed by for me to even have a clue as to what to get. The day was aging, and I was out of time. I found myself in a grocery store buying a $100.00 AmEx gift card. So there I was, late for the bachelor party.

I met up with everyone at the Sunset Marquis Hotel and Villas in West Hollywood. I see someone was doing well for themselves. The party had already begun. I heard music and laughter on the opposite side of the door. I aggressively banged on the door after several attempts in knocking and waiting. A face without a name opened the door.

"Hey, you must be Michael Evans."

"Yeah, that's right."

"Well, don't just stand there. Come in. The party has already started."

The stripper turned off the music. Apparently she finished with her act. With her trench coat on and her equipment held in her left hand, she walked up to me on the way to the door.

"You missed the action, pretty boy, and that's too bad." Her flirtation was welcomed, and I had regretted coming to the party late. I watched her as she exited the room.

"Eyes over here, buddy. That chapter of the party is over, kid. You should have come sooner," Frank said, waving me on to see the twenty-six-year-old Josiah.

"Well, well, well, Josiah. Boy, have you grown, and now you're getting married." Josiah looked at me with his chiseled face, wearing a long-sleeve white cotton shirt, denim jeans, and Converse sneakers. He didn't know if he wanted to shake my hand or hug me. I grabbed him instead and gave a bear hug.

He pulled me away and said, "Has it been three years?" Our conversation took off, but I knew I couldn't kidnap him to get reacquainted since it was his party.

"It's time for toast, comrades," Frank said, already holding up his glass overflowing with champagne. My catching up with Josiah had come to an end since everyone wanted some of his attention. It was, after all, his party.

The celebration continued, and the guys were getting rowdy and drunk. On my way to the bathroom, Frank called out my name, "Hey, Michael!" He handed me an invitation to the wedding. "Now you make sure that you'll be at the wedding. Do not let me wait another three years to see your ugly face."

"So what gives, Frank?" I said.

"What do you mean?"

Frank had always been tough with me, and it never failed every time we met. "You've always had been hard on me. I was never introduced to your soft side."

"Get used to it, kid. I just overcame prostate cancer, and somehow it changed who I am. If you're thinking that I'm a sissy now, you've got another thing coming." I must have been wearing a sad face because Frank said, "Boo! Wake up, kid. I'm over it, and you should be too. I would hug you, but the nickname 'sissy' doesn't sit very well with me." Frank smiled and winked at me, telling me in his own way not to worry. He eventually joined the crowd, and I ran to the bathroom.

On the way out of the bathroom, I exhaled noisily as a sign of relief. I came across several bedrooms until William, Larry, and Joe called me into a room. The guys were some of Josiah's friends from high school. David came behind me, who was a friend of Marianna's from community college.

"Hey, Evans, you don't hang out with us anymore. Are you too good for us since you're a celebrity?"

William's smart mouth had everyone ready to come and attack me. Ever since I lost my job at Cisco Systems, I worked with my father. I didn't have time to hang out, especially when I was hustling to make ends meet. I smiled at William and remained mute, but that didn't mean that I was hungry to beat his face in.

Then David gave it a try. "Hey, Evans, what is that I hear about you speeding down the street to run away from the paparazzi? Is it true that you beat down one of them and sent him to the hospital because he cut you off the road to take pictures? I heard you lost some jobs because of your temper and drinking."

"I didn't know that I was on trial," I said, hoping that it would end.

"Hey, Evans, do you care about what people are saying about you?" Joe said.

On my last entry I said, "No. Just like I don't care that you're pushing drugs into your veins."

"Do you want a taste of some smack?"

"Smack?"

"Yeah, man, smack. It's a street name for heroin. Where have you been, man?"

"Not on smack," I said. Doing something new doesn't mean doing something stupid. "Guys, I'm out."

"Wait, wait, Evans, here's a gift for you." Joe gave me a couple of samples of smack and walked away. I placed it in my pocket and walked out. I thought, *Maybe trying something new doesn't sound so bad after all.*

I rejoined the party with my crew, and as I see it, they were as drunk as they wanted to be. I glided around the bar and poured myself a glass of scotch. There was a knock on the door, and Josiah cleared this path open it.

"Well, hello," Josiah said.

I raised my head up after finding another bottle of scotch. I couldn't believe in what I was seeing at that time.

"Well, hello, Michael. Glad to see me?" It was Claire Heisler, and no, I wasn't happy to see her. She was the last person I wanted to see.

"What do you want, Claire?"

"Can we have some privacy?"

"You can say what you have to say right here. I'm not going to bother in asking you how you found me."

"I want you back, Michael, plain and simple."

The guys laughed as I stood there in shock. What the hell was she thinking? Kyle, one of the guys there, yelled out, "I've heard that Kardon guy dropped you like a hot potato, saying that he didn't need you anymore."

I thought about how ironic that was. It seemed I heard that before. Claire begged me to take her back. She stated that she didn't know what she was doing at the time she dumped me. Every time she spoke, she made me ill.

"Claire, enough," I said. "I don't want you back. It was because of me that you were considered in being in a part of a movie. It was me that you got into some of the clubs. It was because of me that your face was shown to the media. You can start now in getting out of my face."

I couldn't help but laugh while I continued to fill up my glass with scotch. She looked and sounded pathetic. I took a sip of my drink just to look up and see her still there. Claire dug inside her purse.

"What is it now, Claire?" I didn't see it coming. I heard three shots. I fell back in pain until the lights went out.

At first I thought the grave was my new home, but I opened my eyes to a hospital room with IVs placed in all directions. The doctor stood over me and said, "You almost didn't make it, Mr. Evans. All five bullets missed your vital organs. You're a lucky man. We're giving you some blood—you've lost a quite a bit. I'll be around tomorrow to check up on you. Oh, by the way, my name is Dr. Walter Decker. Your father is waiting in the hall. I'll let him in."

The doctor made his exit, and the man I haven't contacted since I was called into the acting job walked into the room.

"Hello son. I thought the next time I heard from you, it would have been, 'Hey, Dad, let's get together.' It hurts me to see you in a hospital or even the thought of visiting you at a gravesite."

My father looked worried, and the only thing I could say was, "I'm sorry." I looked at him and remembered that my father and I have been through a lot together every since my mother passed away. My mother was killed by a car while she was jaywalking from Perth City Hall to her vehicle when I was fourteen. From what I was told, she didn't see it coming. My father did the best he could in raising me, but I could see in his face that he wasn't happy. He worked as a chef in the Perth Hotel and has taught me how to cook one dish to another. It was one day; he confided with me that the memories of my mother saddened him. He explained that she left a mark in the house where they lived for seventeen years, as well as dining in the restaurant where they met and where father worked. He continued to say that it was hard for him to function as a man and father. He then made a proposition to leave Scotland after I was finished with high school to open his own restaurant in L.A. and to make a new life for us. A year after graduating from high school, he did just that. We only had one another, but I managed to bridge the gap in our father-son relationship.

He sat next to me and continued his speech, "Son, listen. I appreciate what you have done for me in sending money in the past years to help the old man, but you have to realize that I would rather see you than your money anytime. If you're embarrassed of me, well, I cannot help that. You have to remember that you too were in the same predicament about four years ago. Nevertheless, the good thing is my pay raise. It raised so much it had this old man doing jumping jacks, cartwheels, flips, and jumping through hoops."

I tried to laugh, but the pain didn't permit me to. My father stood up and pressed the button for some pain medication. I smiled at him and asked him to continue.

He placed his hand on my head and said, "I just need you, so get well enough to get out of this joint. Son, we will not think about the past, just the future."

"I like that," I said. "I like that."

My father didn't stay long after his heartfelt speech, and for a man I hadn't see in four years, I didn't want him to leave. I spent another four days in the hospital, and my release papers were like gold. Keith came to the hospital to pick me up. The ride with him was a little painful. Keith didn't know what to say when I was in agony, so the silence continued to the end of my journey. On that last turn to my house, there were cars resting in the front of the driveway.

"Keith, what's going on?"

"You'll see."

When I opened my door to my home, there was a welcoming team waiting for me. My father and my closest friends held up a welcome home banner and yelled out, "Welcome home!"

It was good to be home. It was good to have a regular meal. Frank and Keith helped me into my bedroom. I wanted to be stretched out in comfort. They included me in on what had happened after I was shot. I found out that little Josiah slugged Claire from behind and put her out until the police and paramedics arrived. Yes, the police placed her in jail and hopefully in prison. There were too many witnesses to polish her story. I was glad I was at home, but I wanted everyone out so I could sleep.

For two weeks, I was popping pain pills like it was going out of style. I called the pharmacy to refill my Vicodin, and the pharmacist refused my request. He said it was too soon to have my prescription filled. I slammed the phone and got up to get dressed. I was going to handle my business with the pharmacist. I put on my jacket and felt something bulky. I pulled out whatever it was and discovered it was a couple of hits of smack. I took off my jacket and tried some to take the edge off. It wasn't long until I found out that this drug was my savior, but I needed more. I called Joe, even though he was a pain. I could use some painkillers now, and I knew he was the one who could help me buy some heroin.

Joe picked me up shortly after the call. "Come on, Michael, are you ready?"

"Yeah, yeah, let's go. Hey, Joe, make sure this stays with us, okay?"

"Not a problem."

The drive was extensive, but the transaction was expeditious. I thought at first, *What am I doing?* but the pain struck a chord. Day after day, I habituated myself in taking my new prescription. Even though I was completely healed, the cravings of heroin overtook my judgment. I would stop at nothing to alleviate the cravings. My actions at the jobsite were a little erratic. The job was almost done in completing the movie *Reflection to Perfection*. It was clear that I was messing up to the point for Mr. Bloomberg to call me to the side.

"Mr. Evans, I have put up with your proceedings for a month. I know you were shot two months ago, but I will not allow you to screw up my progress for this movie. My deadline is around the corner, and I need to finish that last scene! Can I trust you to finish this scene?"

With Mr. Bloomberg's aggressive nature, I knew I needed to act right or be fired. "Yes, Mr. Bloomberg, you can trust me."

On the way to the rest of the cast members, Mr. Bloomberg added, "I'm taking you off any upcoming projects until you prove to me that you're capable of working." Mr. Bloomberg stormed off and announced to the cast to go home and come back tomorrow to finish the last scene.

Between the cracks, I sneaked out without notice. I eased up on the goods that night, which made an impression the next morning. The movie was finished, Mr. Bloomberg was exultant, and I went home to ease my pain. Without any upcoming jobs, I was given an opportunity to act the way I wanted. I hopped to the clubs to party and sowed my royal oats. The next day I was caught with possession of drugs and drunk driving. Boy, from a person who never got into trouble, I now have a police record. I was held in jail over night, but surprisingly released the next day. Being a celebrity, I was cashing in.

Somehow nothing seemed to matter except for me. I had everything I ever wanted in life. I had the money, fame, women, the home, and cars. My simple life and way of thinking had morphed into something wicked.

After I walked through the doors of the police building, I went to retrieve my car, which the people refused to give me. I had no choice but to catch a cab. It was late in the evening, and the cabbies were not friendly in stopping for anyone when it was dark, so I just walked until I got lucky. A guy approached me, asking for change. When I refused, he dragged me along in the alley with his friend who came right behind him and beat the living crap out of me. They took all my money except for the money I had in my shoes for heroin. I stayed in the alley and slept through the night.

I realized when I woke up the next day that I had fallen through the cracks. Instead of using the money to get a ride home, I used the money for heroin because I was in need of a fix. I was high as a kite, and it felt good. My appearance didn't matter to me—my hair out of place, shirt and jeans were ripped with oil stains and blood, and my face probably looked like the express train hit it.

Walking the streets of LA, I needed a drink on one of the hottest days in July. I walked in one of the familiar bars that quenched my everlasting thirst. I had money left from the smack, so I made my home on the stool next to the bar.

"Fill 'er up, Mack." He knew what I wanted and how I wanted my drinks.

"Here's your scotch, Mike."

"Keep it coming, my friend. I have twenties. Oh wait, I found another ten."

"I'll be back, buddy. I need to make a quick phone call."

"Handle your business," I said, falling off the stool on the fourth drink. Mack came back and poured me four more drinks. "Hey, friend, thanks," I said.

"Come on, Mike, let me help you to the table here. I don't think you're able to fall out from this chair."

I was out of my mind. Here I was still high on heroin and drunk, and somehow I knew that I had reached the most pathetic part of my life. I leaned my head against my hand and was working on the eighth shot of scotch. My head became heavier and heavier until I passed out on the table.

Instead of resting, I was taken on a horrific journey. A black veil fell upon my face, and darkness had taken over. I thought it was all over. I figured I croaked and was getting what I deserved. The more I struggled in the midst of darkness, laughter ricochet all around me, which gave me an indication I was defeated and that I should throw in the towel. Anxiety fell upon my heart and into my wrecked soul. This wasn't the place I wanted to be. I continued to struggle in darkness, bound and imprisoned in my life blunders. In the midst of it, I felt someone striking me across my face.

"Wake up, Michael. Wake up, Michael. Wake up. This is Frank, wake up."

I woke up, still drunk. "Hey, Frank, how did you find me, man?"

"Come on, Michael. I don't know how the hell you got yourself into this mess."

In his car, Frank talked and talked, but the language he was speaking was cryptic. The day was long, and it was time for my last hit of heroin that was hidden in my inside jacket pocket. I knew Frank was taking me home, and once that happened, I was on my way to a painless trip. Nevertheless, I was wrong. Frank was navigating me to his house. It was like suddenly I snapped back from being under the influence of alcohol to figure out what was going on.

"Frank, I thought you were taking me home."

"Now who told you that?"

Our short conversation fell into a dead silence.

"Come on, Michael, get out of the car."

Frank seemed to be in a pissy mood, but I wasn't buying it. I wanted to go home, but not in my condition. I wasn't able to deal with Frank. In his home, I told Frank that I needed to use the bathroom. He said okay. Now with my last shot of heroin, I was in the last stages of the process before injecting the good into my veins.

Frank knocked on the door. "Are you okay in there?"

"Yeah, fine," I said. I injected myself quickly, but it wasn't fast enough. Frank busted into the bathroom and caught me red-handed. I forced the rest of the heroin into my bloodstream, and Frank snatched the needle from my arm and threw me into the shower.

"Let's see if you would like a cold shower."

I fought back, and every time I did, Frank hammered me back into the shower. I felt my heart pulsating out of control and wanted the cold water to stop. Frank held me down until I was no longer struggling.

"Get up and change your clothes." Frank followed me into the bedroom and watched me until I was dressed.

"It's like that, Frank? You have to watch me change?"

"Michael, in my mind, I'm cursing the hell out of you. It is because of my sister that I'm trying to hold my tongue. She's a Christian now. I'm sending you to the Canyon rehab place tomorrow. I made an appointment. If you haven't noticed, I didn't ask for your opinion."

The next day came rather quickly, and I wasn't looking forward in going to a rehab facility. I'm not as sick as those people. Frank supervised me in the whole process of getting cleaned up and dressed. I felt so violated.

We were on the road by ten o'clock in the morning to go to Malibu. There were no words exchanged. I had nothing to say. I didn't have time to contemplate what I should do in order to recover from my misfortune. After all, it was my fault in getting in this mess anyway. As an adult, one would think they have rights to their own decision making. Well, I'm afraid it didn't apply to me in this case.

The ride to Malibu wasn't as long as I wanted it to be. Approximately fifty minutes into our journey, we were already on-site. The landscape of the canyon was breathtaking, but the thought of it being in a rehab facility never escaped me.

We met with Thomas Ulrich; apparently he manages the whole facility. The appointment wasn't as long as long as I imagined. Frank and Thomas consulted each other as if they had spoken before. I think Joe ratted me out.

Before signing any papers, Thomas Ulrich asked me the ultimate question: "Do you want to be here?"

After answering questions about my addictions, this was above all the hardest question I had to answer. "No," I said. "I don't want to be here. I'm not sick." With my bag of clothes resting on my right side and looking at the expression on Frank's face, I told Mr. Ulrich that I was going to stay because it was my duty to get well for my family, friends, fans, and myself.

Frank smiled. "Good going, Mike."

I was shown to my room and then given a tour of the facility. Frank left shortly after the tour.

On my first night, I was thirsty. It was not the thirst of alcohol but of heroin. The thirst reached its pronounced level at the end of the day. Louie Armstrong—not the singer—was assigned to me during the detoxing period. Quitting cold turkey, what were they thinking? I couldn't sleep. I was experiencing cold flashes, vomiting, muscle pain, and cravings. I must have said every foul word that was conjured up during the period of mankind. I wanted my smack, and I wanted it now!

Five months later I was resting with my thoughts at the pool when I was interrupted by an older African American man. He was tall and slender. His smile owned both sides of his jaw. Wearing a white cotton suit and brown sandals, he came where I was sitting.

"Mr. Evans, hello."

"Hi, are you a new counselor?"

"You can call me Jacob. I see that this facility has helped you mighty fine, but I'm here to give you something that will help you save your soul."

Confused, I asked, "What are you talking about?"

"I'm talking about God, son."

I cleared my throat. "I'm not interested, Jacob, but it has been a pleasure meeting you."

"Well, Michael, it's not that simple. You see, I was sent by the Big Man himself, and the only thing I'm asking from you is to listen."

"Okay." I didn't know what to expect. I had never seen this man before, yet his presence seemed comforting. I sat back where I was sitting, and he spoke.

"When we respond to our inner desires, temptation is enticed and we sin. You see, Michael, in James 1:14-15, 'But each one is tempted when he is drawn away by his own desires and enticed.' Then when desire has conceived, it gives birth to sin, and sin, when it is full-grown, brings forth death."

What the hell was he talking about? Sin, death, what?

"I lost you, didn't I? Well, my friend, you were drowned by your own desires, and the lust for women was one of them. Your wand was busy making visits into the caves of numerous women. Your desires and temptations had you looking for more. I have a suspicion that you worship money as your modern god, and the only thing I would like for you to see is that you have imprisoned yourself in the sinful nature of this world. But you have to ask yourself: Do I love myself enough not to share my body to every woman who crosses my path but only to a woman I have chosen to be my wife? Do I love myself enough that money doesn't make me but I make it?"

"Jacob, thank you for the talk, but the Bible and your God are asking too much."

"Oh, let me get this right. God is asking too much when He inspired the people to write something like 'do not steal or commit murder, fornication, or adultery'? Come on now. This world is made up of laws that people have to abide to and some of things God is looking for us to do. God is of love and mercy. When we are in need of help, Christ is a cry away. He will lift you up and dry away your tears. Serving God separates us from the people who have chosen to live in the world, meaning lusting over or turning their possessions or daily ritual into their modern shrine. Their god and heaven is on earth."

"Who are you, Jacob, really?"

"I'm just a messenger, Michael."

"I had this dream that I was in darkness and couldn't find a way out. There was not a single soul to help me. I was struggling to break free."

"That was one way in getting your attention, but let me tell you that God will never leave you nor forsake you. If you're willing, say the repentance prayer with me and become a child of God. Admit that you're a sinner and ask Him to cleanse your soul and deliver what is keeping you from Him."

I agreed in saying the repentance prayer because I wanted to have faith that God would delivery me from my addictions. I didn't know how. No one really spoke to me like that. He genuinely cared. I was lost and unsatisfied with my life. Having it all doesn't necessarily mean happiness.

After the prayer, I conversed with him a little more. My skeptical behavior toward Jacob had come to an ease, and I found myself drawn in to what he had to say. Just like most good things, it all has to end one way or another. I noticed that he left his Bible behind, but when I looked up, he was gone.

Days had passed, and I was in my room packing my bags. "Michael, your father is here. He will be waiting for you in the lobby."

"Thanks, J.P. Tell him I'll be out soon."

At the final stage of my departure, I had to take my last look around. On the way to the lobby, I gave the receptionist the Holy Bible.

"Beatrice, a man by the name of Jacob left this behind, and I think he may be one of the counselors here."

"I'm sorry, Michael, we don't have a counselor with that name. The only Jacob who was here died one month ago. I believe he was about twenty-four years old. Beatrice opened the Bible. "I don't know who Jacob you speak of is, but he signed this book for you."

She handed the book back. It never occurred to me that the Bible was a gift. I slipped it in my bag, and I was off to meet my father.

"Son," my father started off while he was embracing me, "let's get out of here."

I was going home once again to a place I had left behind. I was ready to start over. We stopped for iced coffee and talked about old times. I couldn't believe that my lust for fame robbed me of my time with family. Thanks to Jacob, I have an opportunity to make things right.

In a month's time, I stayed focused and drug free. The paparazzi kept me on the headlines for weeks, and the magazine companies helped me get jobs by writing articles about being a changed Michael Evans. My fans increased in numbers, and Mr. Bloomberg called me little over two months after my arrival back home. He invited himself to my home, which I had put up for sale. I had to move on with my life and the crowd that could infect my new stature. I may have been a new Christian, but I wasn't strong enough to withstand the temptation.

"Well, Michael, it's about time. I thought I was going to die of old age."

"You said that it was about time that I got myself together, but I didn't see you helping me. You just stopped giving me jobs and stopped everyone else in doing the same."

"Listen and listen well. I did that to prevent you from further embarrassment. You let pride and the lust for money and women clutter your judgment." We sat down on the sofa. "Frank came to me one day. He wanted to place you into some rehab place. I didn't know how to help you. You were too far gone, so I prayed. I set up an appointment for Frank to meet with Thomas, my cousin. By paying for the rehab up front for their services, I had to trust Frank to get you to Canyon Rehab facility. Thomas pulled a few strings to get you in very quickly. Michael, I don't have to tell you what I've done for you to prove that I was there for you. I just want you to know that I was there for you, and that should be the only thing that really matters."

I had to say something but couldn't. Mr. Bloomberg rose up from his seat to reach for his bag.

"Here, Michael, this is a new script. It is something about you. It's called *Gone and Back Again*. I want you to play the leading role. This will help you, all right?"

I was dying to read the script to see how it could facilitate me. I wondered why he made that remark in the first place.

"I have to go. Any bites on your offer on the house?"

"Yeah, as a matter of fact, two people are interested. I should find out next week who I will congratulate."

"Good luck to you, and see you soon."

I was going on three months, one week, and four days of being drug free. My ex-girlfriend, heroin, was still in town. Although I wasn't attracted to her anymore, my cravings sometimes still lusted for her. I thanked God every day for helping me stay clean for this long, and I knew with His help I would stay clean until death claimed my body. I had faith.

Marianna and I had been dating for four weeks now. Life was good once again. I wanted to surprise her for her love and support in my time of need. I set up a date at a five-star restaurant where Keith and I went and met the bartender who was the owner. Well, the owner had the table and the lights set up for me and my date. The only thing I had to do was to wait for my date to arrive.

I stood on the rooftop, taking in the beauty of the city and the night's fresh air. Suddenly, someone pressed a revolver to the back of my head.

"Give me a reason not to pull this trigger." It was a woman's voice, but it wasn't Marianna's. "You don't recognize me."

"How can I?" I said. "You're standing behind me."

"Turn around, and do it slowly. I'm not up here to play games, Michael."

Well, the day had come to meet up with Maggie once again. I should have known her presence when the foulness of the air appeared.

"Cat caught your tongue? I promise I won't shoot you yet. You're probably wondering why we are at this point, right? Come on and talk to me. When I'm ready to shoot you, you'll be the second to know."

Afraid for my life, I said, "What now? What have I done for you to have a gun to my head?"

"Ah, he speaks—that's better. Now was that hard? Let's see…what's first? Okay, you put my sister away."

My eyes widened with disbelief—I didn't know they were related.

"Oh, don't act surprised. You slept with me and dumped me. Gosh, I felt so used. What, Michael, you wanted to say something?" I couldn't help but think that this woman had lost her mind.

I remembered the day that Claire dumped me when I went to the bar to find her. I got so drunk I didn't know who I was sleeping with. Well, it was when I woke up in her bed, lying next to her that I realized what I had done. I wanted to throw up. I wanted to kill myself for sleeping with the enemy, but instead I walked out of her house half naked and drove off.

"Don't have anything to say, huh, Michael? Well, that's okay. I'll do the talking for now until I'm ready to hear your last plea. Hum, where was I… Oh, there we go. I lost my job because of you. When you decided to testify against my sister in court, my name popped up. You sent my sister to prison for life, and when the word got out, I lost my job. Using men for pleasure is not a crime. So on that note, are you ready to die? You should find yourself with God. I heard that you're a new Christian who was baptized in Bloomberg's church. Now I hear that you're talking to men and women about Christ. Who would have thought that fat bastard was a Christian?"

"Maggie, that's enough."

"Oh, he speaks again. Well, time's up, Michael. Say your last words."

"It's about time."

"See you in hell."

"I don't think so, Maggie." Marianna pushed Maggie from behind, struggling to keep the gun away. I tried to intervene and got shot in the shoulder. The struggle continued until Maggie was hanging from the side of the roof. Marianna backed away, and I tried to help her.

"Maggie, I cannot help you if you don't drop the gun."

"I didn't ask you for your help, you moron."

I tried raising her up with the good arm, but she raised her gun once again and shot me in that same shoulder. I let go of her and fell back. It was then that she fell to her death.

"Please tell me that you didn't date her."

"Does it matter?"

Marianna looked over the edge of the roof. "No. Not anymore. I called the police."

"I hear them now."

Four months later, Marianna and I got married. She was the second best thing that happened to me, next to being saved.

Working on the film *Gone and Back Again* was a challenge that I finally overcame. By acting out my life story, I saw how much I messed up in life. But God came and cleaned me up and gave me a new one.

After wrapping up the last scene, Marianna and I were on our way to an intimate road trip. I was ready.

Mr. Bloomberg said, "Okay, everyone, we will meet again in two weeks. Everyone has done a great job."

The cast lingered around, chatting with one another. I rushed to my bride's side on the way out of the studio. In my Corvette, we dressed the trunk with a blanket, drinks, and a large basket filled with snack goods. With our sunglasses shielding our eyes from the sun, we were off without a destination.

I went through hell to get to this point, and Satan, I'm going to tell.

You see, you can bring a child to a popular toy store and warn that child that they are allowed to choose only one toy. The temptation has already reached its peak and goes into its full capacity. This child has found him or herself a handful of toys.

"Choose only one," the parent would say, but how can you choose if you like them all?

God raised me up and out of the dilemma and curse that I had brought upon myself. Satan, I'm going to tell about the bait you placed out there for the taking. I was tempted with the beauty of the woman's body. It didn't matter what their nationality was—I wanted the taste of them all. I was introduced into fame, and my god was an oversized house, cars, money, fans, drugs, booze, and the celebrities' customer service. My desires wanted it all, and temptation clouded every judgment.

"For what is a man profited," Matthew 16:26 said in KJV, "if he shall gain the whole world, and lose his own soul?" I thought I had it all because I had received what I wanted, but at the same time my soul was lost and filthy with sin. Why would God take a dirty soul to heaven? I knew Satan had his hand out for acceptance for a dirty and lost soul, but I'm glad that I'm saved now. Can you say the same? Keep in mind that you don't have to be a celebrity in order to be saved. This applies to everyone.

Check this scripture out and see if you have fallen in the same predicament as I. I've learned that "marriage is honorable in all, and the bed undefiled: but whoremongers and adulterers God will judge" (Hebrews 13:4, KJV). My lust was out of control. The comfort in being with a woman was satisfying. Who cares if I wasn't married? My needs needed to be met. Celebrities now are fornicating and having families, and they are not even married. People honestly believe that it is okay. Being a celebrity of any kind or an average person doesn't give you a free pass in doing what you want. One must remember that sin is sin.

Try in becoming a Christian; it'll open doors to a better understanding. Even though I am married now, I still remember the shameful act of repeated sin. For the Holy Bible comes back and says, "Love not the world, neither that things that are in the world. If any man loves the world, the love of the Father is not in him. For all that is in the world, the lust of the flesh, and the lust of the eyes and the pride of life is not of the Father, but is of the world." But the comforting part is "...the world passeth away and the lust thereof: but he that doeth the will of God abideth forever" (1 John 2:15-17, KJV). Do you believe in second chances?

Greed. The more money I made, the more I lusted for more. Working for Mel's Diner, I had nothing. Living paycheck to paycheck was how I lived until Mr. Bloomberg came and took all my struggles away. But little did I know that I was on a journey to meet with Christ. Money and fame corrupted me; I didn't have Christ in my life to call upon, just the devil whispering in my ear and my gullible spirit feasting on all that was near. Money and fame ruled me, and I'll bet Satan was clasping his hands together and saying another soul lost, an extra point for me. But little did he know what God had in store for me. The evidence of my sins was revealed in the scriptures:

> Perverse disputing of men of corrupt minds, and destitute of the truth, supporting that gain is godliness: from such with draw thyself. But godliness with contentment is great gain. For we brought nothing into this world, and it is certain we can carry nothing out. And having food and raiment let us be there with content. But they that will be rich fall into temptation and a snare, and into many foolish and hurtful lusts, which drown men in destruction and perdition. Charge them that are rich in this world, that they be not highminded, nor trust in uncertain riches but in the living God, who giveth us richly all thing to enjoy; that they do good, that they be rich in good works, ready to distribute, willing to communicate. Laying up in store for themselves a good foundation against the time to come, they may lay hold on eternal life.
>
> 1 Timothy 6:5-10; 17-19 (KJV)

I drowned myself with temptation, and I was a fool to believe that the world had more to offer than Christ.

Satan has an encrypted mind-set. Darkness follows him as he crosses paths of his victims, which means all of God's creations. It is sad that Satan is still vengeful after all these years when God himself removed Satan from heaven's door. He will stop at nothing in collecting as many people as he possibly can before his time folds for the last time. As for us, it's sad that we are playing in Satan's tantrum game every time we sin.

I dwelled in darkness in fear of what I had become, but I will not allow Satan to defeat me, for the power of God is real and effective. Satan, I told, and I think I've done my very best. You may try to grab hold, to take me back to my filthy mess, but I will not allow heroin to own me, especially when God is with me, helping me pull through your mess. My motto now is: don't do the crime if you cannot do the eternal time in hell.

Behind Closed Doors

Dear Diary,

This is Katalina again. Everyone believes that I've, well, messed up in a big way, and I guess one way or another I did. I went to the doctor last week and had a blood work done for STDs. This would be my second one in four years.

My blood test was given to me today. I had to take the call behind the closed door of my bedroom. The doctor was concerned about the positive results of HPV. It was just four years ago that I was positive for HIV. Yeah, I was irresponsible. My parents didn't even know. I'd made mistakes, but I couldn't take this one. I had to idle away the years until I reached the age of eighteen. This way I was old enough to keep my medical records confidential from my parents. Yes, don't pass judgment, you're not familiar with the terms I have with my parents. I'm now twenty-two years old and finished with college. It's also time to graduate from the world too.

My parents looked at me as a failure at the age of twelve. I was making Cs and mostly Ds at school. To make matters worse, I was caught naked with my boyfriend lying on my bed in my bedroom. I was then immediately dragged to the doctor the next day and had the entire necessary tests done. When my blood results came back negative for an STD, my parents were relieved. I was then slapped with restraints. I was forced to go to a tutor after school. I had to attend sex education classes, meeting outside the school grounds. I was forbidden to sign up in any after school activities, meaning no sports, social events, or any fun. I had to come home right after school. So at that point, I didn't have a life. But at the age of thirteen, I found a way to make myself available to my boyfriend, and no one knew. At the age of fifteen, I had multiple partners; I couldn't keep count. I never felt so wanted and cared for.

My parents were rarely available. My father is a surgeon and my mother a psychologist. Work had consumed them so much it seemed that I didn't have any parents. The only thing my parents were engrossed by was making good grades so that their children would also possess good jobs. Boy, I wonder even now on why they had children. Life was rough for them too, raising three kids and paying half of my older brother's college fund. My brother's scholarship covered the remainder of his expenses. My guy friends kept me company. They showered me with gifts for sex. Who was I to say no? I got the attention I needed. Besides, I see people on television do it all the time. My parental guidance didn't know about my extra curriculum. As long as I was making good grades, I was clear. I was on the honor roll from the time I attended middle school throughout my college days. My family couldn't be any happier with my academics, but I wasn't happy with my life.

I want very much to eradicate the HIV and HPV from within me. I wasn't seeking much treatment for my disease, so it lingered. If I was removed from my parent's home by death, so be it. I just want to suffer anymore than I already have.

My brother, Joseph, is living the life after college as a biochemist. My little sister, Daphina, is starting high school. I hope my parents will spend an efficient amount of time with the baby in the family. I hope she will not turn out like me, wanting the attention.

Dear Diary,

This is my last entry and the life God has given me. I wish there was a better way.

> Earth to earth, ashes to ashes, dust to dust; insure and certain hope of the resurrection into eternal life.

> We can stand here today and claim promises based on God's Word that physical death does not mean annihilation. It does not mean total destruction. Death is not the end of existence.

> Look at the world around us for a clue. Even nature teaches us lessons and reminds us that life goes on and on. What at first looks like the end of a cycle really is not the end of anything but the beginning of a whole new life. What looks like a dying tree and a dying plant is simply a waiting spring. What appears to be a withering flower is but awaiting a new bud. A seed will die in the earth, but a whole new plant will arise from its dying.

> We do not gather here to call attention to the end of anyone's life. Instead, we come here to claim a promise that what is happening before us is not the end of anything but the beginning of an entirely new existence that comes through the belief in our Lord Jesus Christ. It's not an exit but rather an entrance.

> Even though one short step separates us from this thing called death, when it actually occurs, we

discover that death is not what we thought. It is indeed so elusive! Death is not the destructive, totally mysterious force that we feared it to be. Instead, we will discover death to have been conquered already by our Lord who experienced it for himself and then came back to tell us that we should not fear death because he had made preparations for us. "Let not your heart be troubled" (John 14:1).

That is why we are here today to claim the promise made not only to Katalina, a daughter who has passed from this life, but also to all who believe in the name of Jesus.

Let's pray. God, grant us the grace to envision all of life as within your love teach us to rest upon your promise that preparation has been made for now and eternal life. Amen.

Two Years Later...

Hello Dairy,

It's Daphina Chavez again.

I'm now sixteen and finishing up high school. I'm sorry that it has been years since my last entry. My older sister, Katalina, passed away, and I had lost all courage in writing. I was upset with my sister for the longest. It wasn't that she died but how she died. How can someone find the courage to hang themselves? When she was amongst the living, she would have a new boyfriend every week. I thought, *What happened to your last boyfriend? He wasn't good enough for you?* I thought at first she needed a guy to love and cherish, just like Mom and Dad love and cherish each other, but of course I was wrong. Every day Katalina would bring one of her boyfriends in her room before Mom and Dad came home from work. I guess she was looking for some other type of lovin'. The taste of sex for her was like candy, and too much of it will give you cavities. In her case, her sweet tooth gave her an incurable disease, but that didn't stop her. The addiction grew, and so did her chances of living in a grave. I'll make sure that I don't degrade myself like that. My body is my temple, and no man will ever take an advantage of me. I will not use my body for any special perks. My sister had taught me to grow up by her actions. Let her rest in peace.

Ten Years Later...

Now here I stand in a pool of shame. It would be raining on this day. I am laced with shame and resentment for the company I worked for. I stood in the midst of the rain, watching my clothes getting damp, damper, and soaked. I not once grumbled about my clothing nor my hair, just stood in front of my job, watching this old woman sympathize for me. I thought she was a wicked woman who couldn't mind her business, but it was I who was wicked and now depressed.

It was late in the evening, and I wanted to go home. I approached the doors to Devine for Design Advertising Inc., my job and my curse. With the exception of my jacket, I had everything I needed. I turned around and started my journey home. I left my car resting in its parking space and walked. It was ten miles to the Westlake Village Apartments. I took off my three-inch heels and continued to distance myself from the job. From the corner of my eye, I thought I saw the old woman following me, but without an umbrella shielding my body, the darkness and the rain blinded my sight.

"'For what profit is it to a man,' the woman yelled, 'if he gains the whole world, and loses his own soul?'"

"Shut up, old woman. I know now." I started to run. I looked back to see if she was following close behind. She stood there and laughed. I continued to run with my bare feet until I reached the Muni bus stop. I sat and rested.

"James expressed, 'Each person is tempted when he is drawn away and enticed by his own evil desires,'" the old woman said.

The bus picked her up on the opposite side of me. She carried an angry look on her face as the bus drove off. She was right, and I was wrong, but there's nothing I can do about it. I needed my job. You see, I was offering my body to the CEO at my workplace for an exchange to my rightful position.

Two Years Earlier...

Life itself couldn't get any better in what I'm experiencing at this very moment. I just graduated from the top of my class. I've earned a double major in advertising and in graphic design. Now I'm ready to grow my roots into a prestigious advertising company. One week rolled around comparatively fast. I've sent my résumé and letters of recommendation from the previous advertising company to thirty-five companies. I hope they will find a place in the company for me.

A week and a half had passed, and I wasn't receiving any phone calls. *That can't be right.* I marched into my bedroom and changed into my comfortable career wear. My plans were to personally hand in my résumé and the letter of recommendation.

It was getting late in the evening. I wished I'd become conscious to the fact that I could have gotten started on this project sooner so this madness could have been accomplished. But no, I sat on my rump roast until two-sixteen in the afternoon before a lightbulb flashed above my head with an idea. *Ugh!* After visiting twelve companies, the last place for the day was Devine for Design Advertising Inc., one of my preferred places to work. I handed in my golden ticket to the receptionist with a smile and began to walk away.

"Wait, Ms. Chavez?"

"Yes."

"It's 4:47 p.m., and I believe that Mr. Stanten has room for another interview. Are you interested?"

"Yes, of course."

"Just wait in the waiting lounge and I'll let him know that you're here."

"Thank you…um."

"Stephanie, my name is Stephanie."

"Well, thank you, Stephanie."

Wow, my day and hour has picked up. Yes! Okay, okay, remain calm, professional, and focused, Daphina.

"Ms. Chavez?"

"Hum?"

"Mr. Stanten is waiting for you inside."

"Thank you."

For a very short journey into Mr. Stanten's office, it had seemed long and unnerving. I thought I had forgotten how to walk. I kindly knocked on the door.

"Come in, Ms. Chavez."

"Hello, Mr. Stanten. Thank you for this opportunity."

I firmly shook his hand, but I had a little hard time getting it back. I was then asked to have a seat. For ten to fifteen minutes, the interview had gone well. I was waiting for the approval for the entry-level position. I just could feel it down in my bones. I was better and had more experience than the entry-level of advertising, but I was willing to take the offer and work my way up.

I was holding back the excitement when he said, "I'm impressed with your résumé and working skills, but I'm very impressed with the two, three, oh, five recommendation letters. Wow, you were the top of your class. Extraordinary. I can offer you the position as a mail clerk."

"I'm sorry, you said what?"

"A mail clerk position. You're fresh from college, so this is the best position. You can move up sometime this year. Let me see…we're in the month of May. I know you're excited. In this prestigious company, opportunities are made available. So Ms. Chavez, are you interested in being part of this family?"

What happened here? Did someone put me in the fighting ring and knock me out on the first punch? Boy, thoughts were scattered and endless.

"Ms. Chavez, are you okay?"

"Yes."

"Like I said, opportunities will be made available sometime this year to move up in the company, but it is up to you to make that decision. So again, Ms. Chavez, are you interested in working in the mail department?"

"I'm sorry. Yes, I'll take the position. I'm looking forward to working hard so I can move up in this company."

"I'm glad to hear it. You will start tomorrow. Your duties will begin at 8:30 a.m., but I would like for you to come at eight o'clock because of paperwork."

"See you tomorrow at eight o'clock."

"Good, I'm really looking forward to it. Good night."

I went home happy but depressed. I was thrilled to get into one of my favorite companies but depressed about my position. I'd seen Mr. Stanten and how he looked at me. He was probably thinking that I was just another pretty face trying to get a job that was above my means. Did he read my résumé? Did Mr. Stanten forget how to read, or was he too busy looking at me? I am a Latina with long, black, curly hair and an hourglass-shaped body, but I did have a degree. I wondered if I would get some respect. Mailroom clerk, no! To me, it was saying, "No-brain bimbo on aisle one."

The next day, I arrived at the workplace on time—eight o'clock in the morning. I witnessed Richard from my advertising class flying out to the office of Mr. Stanten's in a good mood.

"Oh, Daphina, you work here too?"

"Yes, this is my first day. What gives?"

"I was just given the entry-level position that was posted in the *Chronicle* newspaper. I start today. Mr. Stanten wants to move me up in January. Are you excited?"

"Oh yes, I'm moved." I couldn't show an ounce of enthusiasm. I didn't know if I was selfish or bitter.

"So what are they having you to do? You must be in a higher position than me. Besides, you're the one who was the head of the class. I guess you can say that I was at the rear of the class." He laughed. "I can't believe I got this job. So what is your position?"

I was saved by the yelling executive. "Ms. Chavez, in my office please!"

"I have to go. Mr. Stanten, you understand."

"Oh yes, of course. I'll see you later."

While walking toward his office, I didn't know what to do. I didn't know if I wanted to leave my world-winning position as a mail clerk or slap Mr. Staten around until he screams like a girl for not giving me my rightful position, but I was calm. I smiled as he was handing me the paperwork. He then escorted me to the basement into the mailroom. *Oh, lovely.*

"Whanda!" Mr. Stanten called out.

Whanda looked up and rushed over like a servant. She was a graceful woman who was having a bad hair day. "Yes, Mr. Stanten," Whanda said, exhausted.

"This is your new employee. Make sure she's taken care of."

"Yes, Mr. Stanten."

She greeted me with kindness. I didn't want to let on that I didn't want to be here. I glanced around, and Mr. Stanten was gone.

"Honey, Mr. Stanten doesn't like it here, yet he loves sticking people in the basement."

"Whanda, is there another floor he can use for a mailroom."

"Hon, of course, but that's as far as it has gotten—the idea of it. His motto is 'If it is not broke, why fix it?' Come to my office. You can complete your papers here. When you're done, come and get me, and then I'll show you where you'll be working next."

"Thank you."

Whanda seemed nice. Working here would be manageable until the time came to escape the basement from hell. Filling out paperwork was my relaxing state, but I dreaded what was coming up next.

I stepped out of the office. "Ms. Whanda?" I called out to her.

She looked up and walked her normal pace. I looked at her with a surprised gesture. "Madam, Mr. Stanten is not here, so the roller skate comes off." She looked at me with a smirk and looked over the paperwork to make any necessary corrections. "I'll see that Mr. Stanten received your paperwork, but in the meantime, let me show you around. I expect all my workers to do their job, and the job is sorting, distributing, and picking up mail. If Mr. Stanten is not pleased, he'll get on me, and I'll make sure that I'll get on you. Understood?"

"Understood," I said in agreement. *Boy,* I thought, *this is going to be a long day.* Whanda had a laidback personality, but she meant business.

On my first day, I was planning on calculating on how dreadful my first day would be, but we were so busy I didn't have the time to even calculate a number. At the end of the day, my feet cursed and my body disowned me.

Driving up to my place, daylight stood its ground. I was so tired I closed my eyes for what I thought was only a second. But when I opened my eyes, I felt somewhat satisfied. But the thing was, the sun left me in darkness. It was now eight o'clock at night, and I'd generated enough energy to get out of the car. I shuffled into my place at the Westlake Village Apartments. While running water for my bath, I went into the bedroom and took off my shoes and threw them against the wall.

"Boy, that felt good."

After the bath, I headed into bed. I was too exhausted to be concerned about food, so at 9:38 p.m. that night, lights were out, and I was on the night train to sleep. It was then the phone rang.

"Oh my! I can't get a break. Hello?"

"Hey, Daphina, is this a bad time? It sounded like you were asleep."

"Yeah, but who cares? Why are you calling so late, Joseph? Is everything okay?"

"Yes, I wanted to know about your first day on your new job."

Okay, here we go. This was the time when everything was immobilized. The time, people, birds, the wind—I mean everything. I shouldn't have announced this new job to my brother. I had already entered the twilight zone, but this was getting ridicules. How could I explain to my brother, who was a biochemist, that his successful, top-star, head-of-her-class, graduate of a sister is working in a prestigious company as a mail clerk? *Breathe, Daphina.* I think I felt steam coming from my ears.

"Daphina, did you fall asleep on me again?" I needed to avoid his question. "Daphina!" my brother yelled.

"Yes, yes. I'm awake," I lied. I was never asleep.

"Get some rest, sis. I'll talk to you another time."

"Sorry, Joe, but I think that's best. Good night."

"Good night."

Boy, I got out of that. Can I say touchdown?

Another day had passed. *Please, someone help me.* For three months I was in hell, and somehow I had gotten deeper into it. At work someone called my name while I was doing my gravely duties. I turned around and wanted to pass away into a grave deeper than six feet.

"Hello, Richard."

"What are you doing distributing mail?"

Man, interesting question. I was actually thinking the same thing. "Oh, this? Well, I wanted to know every part of this company." He gave me a strange look, so I continued. "You know I'm an overachiever."

"Well, put that down. I need help with this ad."

"Richard, I can't do that. I'm an overachiever, yes, but I have to finish my task."

"Please, just put the mail down a second. I do need your help." He grabbed me and dragged me across the fifteenth floor.

"Okay, I see your desk. It looks masculine. I have to go now."

"Daphina, come on, stop playing around. I really need your help. You were at the head of the class in college, and your input is desperately needed."

Head of the class? Yeah right. Look where it got me. "So, Nike sports?"

"Yes. I have the slogan, but I need to fit my idea somehow with scenery."

"Okay. So you have a slogan for their sport outfits and shoes. Well, how about the Vernal Falls? You want to sell their product to make the consumers think that their outfits and shoes are so comfortable that people are able to run or walk across the wilderness and waterfalls without compromising their comfort."

"Sounds good, thanks."

"So what department are you—"

"Daphina!" Mr. Stanten bellowed. "I need to talk to you!"

"Sorry, Richard, I have to go."

Mr. Stanten pulled me into a corner. By the looks of his facial expression, he was furious.

"Daphina, I didn't hire you as an entry-level advertising clerk but as a mail handler. I want you to do just that!"

Instantly, I was embarrassed. I needed to get away and hide. I knew my face was flushed during his barking and spitting on my face.

"My apologies, Mr. Stanten. Richard needed my help, and I was the best person to assist him."

"I don't give a—" He cleared his throat. "I don't care. If he is incompetent in doing his job, I'll get the next guy to replace him. Go to work!"

The next guy, huh? I see that I'm never graduating from the basement of this company. My legs trembled when I walked away to retrieve the mail chart. I wanted very much to crawl under a rock and die. Richard looked at me, and he knew. His eyes were filled with sympathy. I never understood why Richard was struggling through college to get a job when both he and his family are wealthy. He seemed to really like it here. I had definitely misjudged him. With my tail between my legs, I continued on with my duties.

From graduating day to the holidays, I'd made it to the end of the year. In the mailroom, every inch of the basement was filled with Thanksgiving décor.

"Daphina!" Whanda cheered. "Happy holidays!"

"Sorry, Whanda, I'm not in a cheery mood."

"That was four months ago, Daphina. You need to snap out of it. As CEO, Mr. Stanten knows you're a hard worker. I tell you what, Paul Clay is retiring, and people are moving up. Just ask the boss about a position. Honey, it doesn't hurt to ask."

"Okay, I'll see what I can do."

"All right, you know you're still under my supervision, right? So get to work." She smiled on the way to her small office. I never understood her cheeriness.

"Hi, Daphina."

"Meya."

"Who sank your battleship?"

"Funny. Anyway, don't worry yourself. I'm fine."

"You have to give it up to Whanda. Rain or shine, she's always wears a smile. You know, Mr. Stanten demoted her, but no one knew why. He placed her in charge here, and that's where she has stayed for fifteen years. I don't know how she does it, but she seems to place a little sunshine in our depressing lives."

"I'm going to see Mr. Stanten about an advertising job. He swept my talents under a rug, but little does he know I'm going to resurrect my credentials and dump it right on his desk. I didn't spend money on school to become a mail woman, no offense."

"Please, girl, none taken. I'm finishing up some classes to become a medical assistant. At twenty-six, I don't want to look at mail as being my life story. It took me five years with a daughter to care for to finish school. Next year I'm leaving this prison on good behavior. Can you believe that Mr. Stanten only gave me a two-dollar raise over the past six years? Yeah, he has heartbreaking good looks for a man in his late forties, but he's a little old-fashioned and cheap. He doesn't show much respect for women in a professional level."

"So you're saying I should give up on the idea of demanding a job in advertising?"

"No, no, I'm not saying that, but word to the wise, don't get your hopes and dreams dancing upon the midnight star."

"I'm getting the job, Meya. You just wait and see." I walked off and started to work.

It was now five-thirty in the evening, and I was headed to the sixteenth floor. I was tired. My feet ached. I had a headache. My whole body ached. When the elevator opened its doors, I immediately began to panic. My body became crippled, but I managed my way to his office door. Before knocking, I made a detour to the woman's bathroom to freshen up. Refreshed and secured—boy, I sound like a commercial advertising a deodorant product—I finally conjured up the nerve to knock on his door.

"Come in!"

On second thought, I think I've change my mind.

"I said come in."

Okay, here goes. "Hello, Mr. Stanten. I do apologize in troubling you at this hour."

"No apologies. Just get on with it."

"Okay, I'm interested in the upcoming job that will be available in January. With my recommendations and my résumé displaying my experience, I am more than able in doing the job."

"Daphina, thank you for your interest, but I have Jeff, who is also good for the job. Is there anything else?"

"As a matter of fact, yes. I've chosen this company because it has a good reputation. With my outstanding résumé, you've placed me in the mail department. I've worked there for over six months because I wanted to be part of this company. I deserve my rightful position, sir." I stepped back from his desk and swallowed hard. I was certain that I was going to be permanently dismissed from my obligations.

"Normally, Daphina, I would have fired you, but I have to say that you have spirit. If I give you this advertising position, what would you do for me in exchange? Completely off the record, you see."

"I don't know what you're saying."

He sat far back in his chair with his arms crossed, wearing a smirk on his face the size of Texas. "You're a smart girl—you'll figure it out. But if there is a slight chance that you're not able to, well, then the job goes to Jeff."

I stood there in shock. I couldn't believe his proposal. Mr. Stanten wasn't the CEO of the company after all but the devil in a concealing outfit. I made sure my negative thinking didn't bleed through my facial expression. The thing was, I needed more money. The rent had gone up, and I wanted my rightful place in the company. This handsome male chauvinist pig was my roadblock to success. I needed to blossom in this company so I would be able to move on and forward in my career. I was no fool. I knew what Mr. Stanten was suggesting. But the thing was, did I want to take the bait of a mistake that could destroy me in the future?

"Okay, I'll do it."

"Welcome to Devine for Design."

Mr. Stanten got up and stood in front of me. He gave me a smile of contentment. He walked toward me, and I backed away until I was leaning against his desk. He raised his right hand under my skirt, rubbing against my thighs, and kissed me. I immediately felt ashamed. Behind these closed doors, I hoped no one would ever know that I sold my body to the devil.

When I got home, I stripped off my clothes and took the hottest shower known to mankind. I left my skin red and irritable, yet I still felt dirty. I didn't want to return to work, but I'd made my bed in a verbal contract, and there was no way out.

It was the next day. I didn't know if I should rot at home and dwell in the pool of shame or just suck it up and move on. It was six-thirty in the morning, and my brain activity was on overdrive. I took a shower after I set up the coffeemaker to brew a single cup. After a sip or two of coffee, I was energized enough to put on my work clothes. With a cup of coffee resting in my hand, I was on my way to work.

"Daphina, over here."

"Meya, you wouldn't believe it, but I got the job."

"Come again?"

"I got the job."

"Wow, you must had made quite an impression. I'm happy for you."

"But the thing is, he wants me to work on an account that is close to impossible."

"Girl, you wanted the job, so what's the problem? You can do it. So when do you get started?"

"After Thanksgiving. I thought it was going to be later than sooner."

"And you're still complaining?"

"Okay, point taken. I think he wants me to get started on this Oracle account ASAP. He said he wanted this account before Christmas."

"Wow, and the story continues on. I'm proud of you, but I do have news as well. I have a job. I'll be working at Kaiser Hospital. The yearly income to me is very honorable. That is really all I wanted for myself and my daughter. After Thanksgiving, I'm giving my three weeks' resignation notice. My employer wants me to start work the first Monday in January. I'm glad my journey here is coming to a close."

Overhearing our conversation, Whanda intervened. "And on that note, you girls need to get back to work. Now!"

We quickly exchanged numbers and departed from Whanda's rage.

It was the day before Thanksgiving. I was looking around, grasping every memory of this place. My car was suited up for travel to Santa Barbara. The family wanted to get together once again at my grandmother's place that night while breath still lingered in her body. My grandmother brought joy into our family with her wisdom, love, and sense of humor. She was a Christian woman, and I admired her even though I didn't share the same commitment as she.

Meya took me out on my last day. We went to a restaurant that I never heard of. In San Francisco, there are many tasteful restaurants to choose from, and my friend so happens to find an expensive one.

"Meya, I'm not dying here. You don't have to do this."

"Girl, shut up and get yourself in the restaurant."

I walked into a bistro-type restaurant and stumbled upon the crew from work standing around with balloons and smiles. I didn't know if my fellow coworkers were ecstatic that I was departing from my current position or celebrating the next stage in my line of duty. My thinking process carried cruel speculations and decided to waste the idea.

Whanda started off with her speech. With our drinks held high, she said, "Even though you're moving up, we want to show our gratitude in what you've brought to the job and in our lives. Cheers."

I didn't know what to say, so I said nothing. I was moved by her speech. The position in the mailroom, I wanted to break away from it all, but I never knew that I was leaving behind a magnificent family. I expressed thanks to everyone who attended the party and told them that they could never be replaced from my mind and my heart.

Lunch had come to an end in blink of an eye. I wanted very much for the day to last more than it did.

Reminiscing on my upcoming events, I knew after the holidays that Mr. Stanten would place an order for his evening snack on a daily basis. This was something that I was not looking forward to.

It was an hour before departing from my famous job in the mailroom. I was already feeling the anxiety of losing my family. Wrapping up for the day, Mr. Stanten came unannounced.

"Please don't stop working on my account," he started off. "I want to wish everyone a safe Thanksgiving. I'll see all of you on Monday." On the way out of the mailroom, he added, "I'll see you early on Monday, Daphina, to go over our contract. You know what I mean." He winked at me and continued his departure. My body shivered with the touch of his whisper.

When the big hand circulated the clock once more, it was time to head off to Santa Barbara. I made certain that hugs were passed around to the crew before breaking the speed limit into the congested route to my destination. On the way out, Whanda waved me on.

"You don't mind if I walk you to your car?"

"No, not at all. What's on your mind?"

She paused, and then said, "I want you to be careful on your high-rising career. The person who helped you get where you're going can also help you go down where it all began. Some smiling faces hold nothing but deceit."

What the... What is she talking about? I didn't have time for this. "Okay, Whanda, I'll make sure that I keep that in mind."

"I'm sure you will. If you ever need to talk, I will not be hard to find."

I didn't know what that was about, but I was getting a little paranoid with my extra curriculum behind closed doors. I smiled and thanked Whanda for her advice, but it was time to get on the road. My parents believed in promptness when going to my grandmother's home tonight, so I knew I wasn't allowed to sleep when I got home.

I hadn't seen or spoken to my parents in months. It was last August when I had my last encounter with my parents. I had no regrets. My behavioral reasoning in not communicating with them was authentic. They angered me when I revealed that I was working in the mailroom in an advertising firm. They criticized me and addressed their disappointments. They said I could do better, and when I thought that it couldn't get any worse, they shifted all their attention on my brother and his family. The entire weekend I was invisible. I was a failure. They didn't notice my absence when I drove back to San Francisco. They had the audacity to call a week later to say they noticed that I had left and asked when I was going back. How could I respond to that? Many times I wanted to ask God, *Can I exchange my parents for more enhanced ones?*

The day before Thanksgiving, I was doing my daughterly duties in driving to my parents'. The only desire that I carried on my journey to Santa Barbara was to see my grandmother. At the age of eight-five, she was my light in my darkness and love during my depletion of it all.

I drove up into my parents' driveway with shame still resting on my shoulders, but the outcome of it all would be my parents. They could finally be proud of me now. They would probably say, "Ah, an advertising job in exchange for sex? Wow, baby girl, now that's using your brains." But let's be real. I would probably be the next murder victim in Santa Barbara.

I rang the doorbell and then continued to unload my luggage from my car. The door opened as I was making my way back to the car.

"Hi, Daphina," my mother said. "You've made it." Yelling back into the house, she was chopping away at my father. "Carlos, stop eating those cookies. ... Yes, you are. I can hear you closing the cookie jar. Daphina is here, Carlos. Please help her with the luggage."

"Thank you, Mom."

"Come on in, chica. Come to the kitchen and let's talk."

The first thing that came to my mind was that she knew what was going on. I don't know how, but somehow she knew. She was the kind of woman who was able to look at you and know something was not right. Growing up in this house was nothing but discipline, getting good grades, and, oh yes, *don't turn out like your sister.* Well, I guess some things don't change. I wanted so much for my mother to be proud of me. My academics were one thing, but finding a promising career was another.

With a mug of hot cocoa with marshmallows and a cinnamon stick and my mother's irresistible pecan pumpkin cookies, I shared with them my new position at Devine with Design. Of course, she was proud of me; she couldn't stop moistening my cheeks with kisses.

"I'm always proud of my kids," my mother started off. "I don't always show it, and I do apologize." She rose from her seat and took hold of the mugs and saucers, then walked to the sink. She lowered her head and said, "I just want you and Joseph to be happy." She turned around carrying tears in her eyes until she wasn't able to carry them any longer.

I rose up from my seat to embrace her. I didn't know what she was going through, and I didn't want to pry, but I wanted to make it known that I loved her.

"Muchacha, sit please. We don't have much time. Your grandmother is expecting us in an hour for dinner."

I didn't know how to take her. She had been out of character ever since I walked through the door. I hoped everything was in place with her.

"Daphina, you've probably have noticed that I've changed, and it is because I found Christ. He's has always been there, but I've realized it and woke up to the fact that he is my Lord and Savior."

Wow, I didn't expect that. "I'm happy for you, Mom."

"We found a church—"

My father interrupted her. "No, that church on National Drive, you won't see me in that church. The people in that church need more help than the people outside the church."

"Carlos, please *shh*, just sit with me! Now Daphina, I know your father and I weren't always there for you and your brother. We allowed work to consume our whole existence, and I know it wasn't fair."

My father continued. "We just want to let you kids know that we are here for you now. We cannot make up the past, but we sure can do something now."

I saw right then that my visit with my parents was going to be an unforgettable one. Even though my parents didn't force God on me, I could see the effect he had on them. I wished Katalina was alive to live and breathe the new Mom and Dad.

The night rose, and then the day intervened when I woke up at nine o'clock on Thanksgiving Day. The fragrance of breakfast managed to spread its wings and fly throughout the house.

"Daphina," my mother called out, "come down and have some breakfast with us. Don't worry about taking a shower. You can do that later."

Breakfast was simple, and it was a good thing—a glass of orange juice, Mexicana scrambled eggs, English muffins, and sausages. I wasn't apprehensive in eating. Thanksgiving is a major holiday, and I knew my mother and grandmother were going to cook a major feast. The turkey was already in the oven, and after breakfast I headed up to clean my producing body odor.

Dancing in the kitchen with my mother, preparing this evening feast, the day almost slipped by me. My grandmother, brother, and his family arrived around four o'clock in the afternoon, and my mother and I were just finishing up dinner. Sheena, my brother's wife, assisted us in dressing up the dining room table while my grandmother was placing her famous dishes in the kitchen. My grandmother loved using her kitchen and keeping her recipes a secret.

It wasn't long before the family swarmed around the table. My father said grace over the Thanksgiving feast. For the first time in my life, this home was transformed into a tranquil environment. The spirit in this house welcomed me in love and kindness. Going back work wasn't something I was looking forward to.

I've enjoyed being surrounded with family, but a conspicuous reality awakened my perception of things. It was now Saturday afternoon, and traveling back to San Francisco was on my agenda. While loading up my car with my father, Joseph stopped us.

"I'll take the bags, Dad. I need to talk with sis."

"Okay, see you two inside."

"So big brother," I said, "what's on your mind?"

"Is this everything?"

"Yes, pretty much. I'll come back with the rest of my things during the Christmas holiday, so stop ignoring the question. What's on your mind?"

He scared me when he said, "You know that I'm your brother, right?"

"Right. Come on."

"The last time we spoke, you never called me back. The last time you spent the weekend up here, you were ignored and ridiculed about your profession. People who experienced what you experienced would take drastic measures to please others. I have a brother's sense that you had done something like that. I want to tell you to do what makes you happy and not what makes us happy."

I couldn't say absolutely nothing. It seemed he had entered into my world of pain just to say that it was okay. I couldn't reveal to him what I was doing. He would lecture me and disassemble Mr. Stanten. I didn't know God, but I did thank him in changing my family. Somehow I didn't feel alone.

"Daphina, you don't have to say anything. I'm just a phone call away."

"I really do appreciate that. Thank you."

"Well, let's see what Dad wants before you leave."

"Okay."

Walking back to the house, I said, "All right, Mom and Dad, I have to go. I will see you next month."

Our father popped his head out from the kitchen. "You kids come into the kitchen."

Our parents had a basket of food to take with us. Our father stood tall, wearing a smile on his face with his arm around my mother's waist. My brother made an attempt to pick up his basket, but our mother slapped his hand.

"What?" he questioned.

"We are going to pray first before you two leave. You both have some serious traveling."

Our mother prayed—it was beautiful. We took hold of our baskets and were headed home. I couldn't believe my brother traveled an hour just to say "see you later." He was much older than I was, and we didn't have the bonding relationship like most siblings with close ages. When I was going to middle school, he was starting college, but I'm glad we had started a close relationship four years ago. He's a nice guy.

I was going home to Satan's lair. I was returning to San Francisco. Going home had its perks: I was going home to take a nice bubble bath. After a long trip, this was something I was anticipating—my unforgettable reward.

It was Monday morning. I inhaled and held it for several seconds before releasing it when opening one of the doors to the company. I didn't know if I should be glad or sad, but I knew this was the day that I didn't have to go to the basement.

Oh, the sweet sound of traveling to the fifteenth floor. I stepped out of the elevator and marched across the room and to the location of my desk. Mr. Stanten was kind enough to leave a voice message on my cell to verbally tell me the location of my workstation—near the window. I was already satisfied. My assignment was already resting on my desk. I guess Mr. Stanten didn't want to waste any time.

Wearing my favorite gray pant suit and low-heel pumps, I was ready to work. There was a letter on my desk briefing me on this company called the Oracle Enterprise. I read faithfully until Mr. Stanten arrived with a smirk on his face. I thought it was time to please him behind closed doors, so I stood.

"Oh no, sit, please. I see you didn't waste any time in getting your feet wet."

Ignoring his flirtatious moves, I said, "Thank you, Mr. Stanten, for the literature on the Oracle Enterprise, but I have to say that this is out of my league. We are an independent company, so why do we need help on the outside?"

Mr. Stanten smiled. "Yes, we need some help. This company needs financial stability. I'm looking for a proposal, and the assignment has your name on it. They are not taking over but assisting. So what I need you to do is design and help in advertising a new clothing line for LeAnna. We can use our current success story to show that we are a promising company to sustain. This is your project. Oh, she's expecting your call, okay? I know you can do this. And by the way, I'm expecting to see you in my office tonight."

I wasn't in the mood in pleasing my boss that way, but it was the only option I had to get what I wanted. My brain that day was incompetent. I still didn't get it, so I called the Oracle Enterprise and spoke with Candace. Candace already knew the current situation and assisted me in scheduling an appointment. I had three weeks to conjure up an advertising fad. LeAnna Danielsen was a new clothing designer with a fresh clothing line, and by the looks of it, working with her was going to be fabulous.

For two weeks I couldn't sleep. Coffee and doughnuts were my only stimulant in staying awake and alive to survive. So much for my figure.

A couple of days had passed, and I was able to complete my task to present to LeAnna, but first it had to go through Mr. Stanten. It was December 18, and most of the staff had gone home for the evening. I called Mr. Staten to conclude the final touches of my current presentation. It was ready to go. We met in the conference room and went over the entire presentation. If Mr. Stanten was one of the players in a poker game, he would have lost every hand, because he would unintentionally reveal his hand with facial expressions.

"I'm very impressed with your work, especially for a short time span." He seemed surprised. "I'm putting you on tomorrow. You can show LeAnna your progress, and hopefully we can shoot this ad first thing in the morning."

"Great." *I think.* I was taken off guard. *Hold mule, you're going too fast.* He closed the door to the conference room and locked it, and then I knew.

"Daphina, let's change that meeting to nine o'clock. There's one thing I need you to do before you leave tonight." He began to unbutton his shirt, and I wanted to cry.

It was now Friday, and I was excited to meet up with LeAnna again. It was nine o'clock in the morning, and the presentation began in the conference room as scheduled. The CEOs and the executives from the company were there as well as LeAnna's people. The room held a nightmarish atmosphere, but I was hoping that the success of this presentation would cure it.

I held the meeting for half an hour. I hid my stage fright during the presentation and hoped that no one would notice it.

After the presentation, questions and answers were exchanged, and LeAnna was excited. My first assignment was finished, and nothing needed to be changed. Now the AD was going to be placed on the Internet, TV, and bulletin boards.

Now I was headed back to my desk. I gave Claudia, secretary of the Oracle, a fax of my presentation. We went over it on the phone. I didn't understand why at that time I needed to consult with a secretary of the president in why she should help finance our company. I should be talking to someone higher, but in this line of work, you don't ask questions, you do it, and so I did.

I had to conjure up a story as to why our company could be a great asset to them. Claudia seemed pleased and wanted me to join Mr. Stanten in his office. I was scared at first, but I was doing something that was beyond my ability.

Mr. Stanten stood as I walked into the office. "Daphina, please come in." I knew right then that I was fired. "I have Claudia on the phone, and we agreed to move you up from the entry-level position to a more secure position."

"Okay, thank you, Mr. Stanten and Claudia, but I have to say that I'm confused."

"Let me explain," Claudia volunteered. "There was never a premeditated thought in strengthening the company's financial crises. For what I had been told, Devine for Design is financially stable."

"Extremely stable," Mr. Stanten added.

"Mr. Stanten wanted to test your skills before promoting you. Congratulations, Daphina."

"Thank you, Claudia, but the work I've done for LeAnna, was it a test?"

Mr. Stanten stepped up to the plate. "No, not at all. That was real, and the AD will be shown on the Internet, TV, radio, etc."

"Talk to your later, Steven," Claudia said.

"Okay, Claudia. Thanks again."

Now we're alone. Someone help me.

"Now that we're alone, you can congratulate me properly. If we have time, I'll show you around your new office and your new position." My boss disgusted me, but I didn't have a choice. I loved my job.

It was now Christmas Eve, and I was finished giving Mr. Stanten his early Christmas present.

"Keep up the good work," he said. "I can't believe you gave a knockout presentation to the Oracle Enterprise. You're talented in more ways than I expected." Mr. Stanten pulled up his pants with satisfaction, and I left the office with disgust.

"Daphina," someone called. I looked around to find Mr. Stanten's wife standing in the hall, prepared to greet me. "Daphina," she called again with a sweet voice. "I heard that you were responsible for giving a sensational presentation to the Oracle. You would have had to impress the company quite a bit."

"Thank you, Mrs. Stanten, but it was only to test the potential I have with this company."

"Honey, are you okay?"

I wanted to say *no, because I'm sleeping with your husband,* but instead, I said, "Yes, I'll be fine."

"That answer will do for now, but if you need to talk, you know how to find me."

"Thank you, Mrs. Stanten. I do appreciate the invitation."

We went our separate ways. I was on my way to the car. Santa Barbara, here I come!

"Daphina," someone called. *Oh God, what now.* "Daphina, wait."

I dreadfully turned around. "Richard, you're still here at this late hour?"

"I needed to follow up on a few things. Are you spending Christmas alone?"

"No, I'm heading to Santa Barbara."

"Well, if you have time, I would like to take you out to lunch one day."

"I'm sorry, are you asking me out?"

"I believe I didn't stutter." He smiled.

It was nice being with someone around my age group who was gorgeous and saw me as an individual and not as a play toy.

"Yes, I would like that."

He kissed me on my cheek and wished me a Merry Christmas. I exchanged the same wish and drove off into the night.

On New Year's Eve, the company held a party celebrating the end of 2008 and welcoming the coming of 2009. The idea wasn't mine in coming to the party; Mr. Stanten just wanted someone to ride on that night. Clear across the room, Richard stood and winked at me. So far he was the only spark in this party. I was on a short leash and making my new relationship with Richard known to the company would end my career. As I watched Richard from across the room, Mr. Stanten snuck up behind me and whispered into my ear, "Meet me in my office in ten." He wasn't asking but demanding.

After the meeting with the boss, I went to the restroom and cleaned all the necessary places on my body before rejoining the crowd. It was an hour before we buried 2008, and before the countdown, I snuck off. I caught the bus to work, so walking home will be my transportation, but for that moment, I wished I had driven my car.

"Thou shalt not commit adultery," an older woman yelled from across the street.

"What?"

"Thou shalt not commit adultery!" It angered her to repeat the phrase, and she started to say something else. "'Let marriage be held in honor among all, and let the marriage bed be undefiled, for God will judge the sexually immoral and adulterous,' Hebrews 13:4," the woman said.

"Mind your business, old woman." *My goodness, how can she know?*

She blurted out, "'Flee from sexual immorality. Every sin a person commits is outside the body, but the sexually immoral person sins against his own body.' Read that, child, in First Corinthians 6:18." It seemed that I was being attacked by biblical scriptures. I thought she was finished when she said, "'If we confess our sins, He is faithful and just to forgive us our sins and to cleanse us from all unrighteousness.' That's in First John 1:9."

"Enough, old woman. I don't believe in that mumbo jumbo, so save your lectures for someone who cares."

At first I thought I had accomplished my mission in shutting her up. She frowned at me and stomped her cane onto the pavement. Did I crush her feelings? I didn't care. I continued walking until I heard a bus rushing to my aid. I glanced at my watch and discovered that it was New Year's Day. My bus was approximately three blocks away, and with a smile on my face, I'd waited patiently for it. The old woman, on the other hand, was still haunting me with her stare. She pointed her cane at me.

"'Food is meant for the stomach and the stomach for food, and God will destroy both one and the other. The body is not meant for sexual immorality, but for the Lord, and the Lord for the body,' First Corinthians 6:13." The nightwalkers stood and watched from the sidewalks and some on the streets. I got mad. The bus was one stop behind.

"Old woman, my business is not of yours. Stop haunting me! Save your lectures! Stop being disturbed because your sexual functions are no longer desirable to men. Your troubles are not of mine, and my business is not of yours."

The crowd applauded, and the bus was finally in motion to reach the bus stop. Before the bus arrived, the old woman threw her cane at me, nearly hitting me on my face.

The bus stopped, and the driver said, "I saw that. Do you need some help?"

"No thanks. You just helped me."

"I didn't know an older woman at her age could throw like that. She's about eighty-six to ninety years old."

"Amazing, huh?"

"Well, you're in safe hands now. Where are you headed?"

"The Westlake Apartments."

"When your stop comes, I'll wait until you're in the vicinity of the place. Too many crazies running around, you know."

"Thank you. You're very kind."

"Not a problem, ma'am."

The bus driver was a man of his word.

At home, I took a scalding shower. Every time Mr. Stanten touched me, I always did my best to burn any memories of his touch.

After the shower, I made an unpremeditated move—I drove to Meya's place. I knew she was having a small New Year's gathering at her house. She was surprised to see me at her doorstep. She guided me into her bedroom as her guests got rowdy with booze and music.

"What brings you here? I thought you were going to a party at your job."

I explained what had happened last night and my first day working with Mr. Stanten. She was the first I told about this horror. Her jaw dropped, and she became speechless. After that point, she urged me to quit, but I wasn't having it.

"This is wrong, Daphina. Tell him *no* next time."

"I love my job, and I'm afraid of losing it."

"But you're not afraid to lose your dignity?"

She was right; I had nothing else to say. I stayed for a while before returning home.

It was the January 5. Monday morning was always tough for me. Mr. Stanten didn't waste any time in making his presences known in my office where the door was closed, keeping people in suspense.

"Don't stand," he said. "It is too early for that."

Excuse me? I thought.

"I came here to let you know that we are traveling to Washington, DC. We have a new client who is in need of some assistance. We're leaving tomorrow morning. Just meet up with me in the lobby, let's say around eight-ish, okay?"

The idea in being on a field trip with him was unthinkable. "Okay," I finally responded, placing a smile on my face like I really cared. I knew I was going to be his undercover whore for the next three days in DC, comforting.

Just before lunch, depression fell upon me about the older woman and her true accusations. I didn't love Mr. Stanten but cared about Richard. I entertained the thought about the older woman until I was interrupted.

"Ms. Chavez?"

Moving out of my daze, I said, "Yes? Oh, hi, Ami. How is Whanda?"

"She's doing well. She asks about you from time to time."

"You can let her know that I'm fine."

"I'll tell her, but it would be nice if it came from you. Oh, I almost forgot. I have a letter for you."

"Okay, thanks, Ami, and next time call me Daphina. I'm the same person who worked with you last year."

"All right. Bye, Daphina."

"Be seeing you, Ami."

The letter Ami delivered just had my name on it; there was no return address. I opened the letter to kill the suspense. It was Richard. He wanted me to meet him at the Rainforest Restaurant now. It was noon. I rushed out before someone stopped me to do a task.

Richard smiled when I was escorted to his table. He greeted me with a kiss. "I'm glad you were able to make it."

"Well, I literally ran out to my car. If I didn't know better, I think someone knows about our relationship."

"If they know, so what? I still don't understand why you want to keep this a secret from our workplace."

"Someone at the office could be threatened about the whole thing, and—"

"So what? If this guy cannot—"

"Wow, how do you know it is a guy?"

"I'm just saying, okay. What are you hiding?"

"If you don't mind, I'd rather not say. Please, I want to enjoy our lunch together, all right?"

Lunch started off bumpy, but it didn't really matter to me how things started off—it was all in how it ended that I was concerned about.

After lunch, I entered the doors of Devine for Design. It suddenly lost its charm.

"Hey, Stephanie. Do you ever take a break?"

"A break? What break? Oh, a woman with the name of Meya has been waiting for you in the lobby."

"Thanks, Stephanie."

I met up with Meya and headed to the elevator. Inside, she didn't say a word, and neither did I. I could tell that she wasn't able to dismiss the idea of Mr. Stanten getting away with his pleasurable moments.

Alone in the elevator, she said, "Daphina, if you can only get me alone with this man, I can help finish with your problem."

"Help me how?"

"You see this here?" she pulled out a pocket knife with a blade of the size of my hand.

"Meya, put that away."

"If I can get close to him, I can cut his log off and burn it into my fireplace. He can forget about reattaching his family gems."

"If we weren't in the elevator alone, we would be in handcuffs."

"Girl, relax."

The elevator door opened, and we continued to talk about options and legal actions. I opened the door to my office and saw Mr. Stanten sitting at my desk.

"Mr. Stanten, what brings you to my office?"

"Oh, nothing at all. I see you're getting prepared for tomorrow's trip. Make sure you have everything you need. So if you'll excuse me, I'll get out of your way so you two can talk." Mr. Stanten winked at me as he escorted himself out of the office.

"What was that? A booty call gone bad?"

"Meya, enough."

We sat down on the two chairs facing the desk.

"Daphina, listen, get out now before it's too late. Your job shouldn't be that important for you to sacrifice your body and your dignity."

"I have been looking for another job that fits my criteria, but I have been too busy to set an interview."

"Have you ever heard of calling in sick?"

"I see your point."

"Um-hum, good. I have to go. Go on your business trip and make something happen when you return."

We hugged each other, and she was gone. From my top-left desk drawer, I retrieved my résumé and cover letter and faxed it to the Oracle, T-Zone, and Siesta Inc. I then looked over through the roller index to retrieve the addresses to each company and mailed together the résumé and cover letter. One way or another, I was getting another job.

Preparing myself for the meeting tomorrow in DC, I again lost track of time. It was seven o'clock, and I was rushing to my car to get home.

"So your name is Daphina, isn't it, child?"

Oh no, not the old woman again. I had to pack for a three-day trip. "What do you want now? You want to torture me with your scriptures? Go ahead, I'm leaving."

"'I say this, you young mule,' in Galatians 5:16, 'but say, walk by the Spirit, and you will not gratify the desires of the flesh.'"

"You don't know what you're talking about, old woman. You just don't know."

That was the last conversation we had that night. I spun off from the parking space so fast I almost endangered myself by hitting a parked vehicle. I went home. All my career outfits were hanging on one side of my apartment to the other, and since I hadn't decided what to wear, all my outfits were possibilities.

The very next day, I had my bags packed and all my possibilities still hanging around my apartment. With no time to spare, I threw four potential outfits in a suitcase and flew out the door. While I was on the road, Richard called to wish me luck with my first business trip. He was still adamant in exposing our one-month dating spree, and for once, I didn't care if he shared it to the world. People are responsible for their own actions, and I refused to hide my happiness for the sake of my boss or coworkers. The employees in Devine for Design, they were a type of pig who waddled in slop. They loved to thrive in getting their hands dirty in gossip, creating confusion and problematic situations. What made matters worse, their scheme burned and devoured what it touched. This was a homemade formula where mess is created and released into the atmosphere. I was counting on my résumé, along with my work tactics, to get me out of this company.

At 7:55 a.m., I was hauling my luggage to work. Mr. Stanten was waiting in the lobby, glancing at his watch.

"Good, you're on time. Our ride is here."

"Mr. Stanten, I didn't see anything on the way in."

"The limousine is our ride to the airport." The driver placed our luggage in the car. I glanced back to wave

Stephanie a farewell, but I noticed she was on the verge of crying.

As Mr. Stanten approached the limousine, Stephanie came around from her work station and said, "Be careful, Daphina."

The driver interrupted us. "Ma'am, we're ready to go."

"Okay. I'm sorry, Stephanie, but can we talk when I get back?"

"Sure, honey, don't let me stop you from your trip."

"Ma'am," the driver said once again, "we have to go."

"I'm ready."

In the limo on the way to the airport, Mr. Stanten was mute. I didn't know whether to be frightened or gracious.

At the airport, we were escorted outside on the other side of the airport. It had seemed that Mr. Stanten had his own private jet, fueled and ready for lift off. During our flight to DC, he remained mute. The only words that escaped from him were *yes, no* at times, and *excuse me*. The journey was pleasant. No one asked anything from me. For once I was treated like a queen. The pampering treatment continued on as the limo driver in Washington, DC, opened our doors for entry. The trip to the Hilton Hotel was remarkable. I was able to glance at the sights, but once again, Mr. Stanten remained silent.

Don't do me any favors, I thought. *I'm having a good time.* I shadowed Mr. Stanten to the front desk of the Hilton Hotel. *For once I'll have some privacy until the meeting tomorrow.*

"Yes, may I help you, sir?" the person at the front desk asked.

"Yes, I have reservations under the name James Stanten."

"Okay, Mr. Stanten, I see here that you have reservations for two for the executive suite with queen-sized bed. Would that be correct?"

"Yes."

"All right. I need for you to sign here, and the card key is yours. The bellboy behind you will follow you to your room with your luggage. Enjoy your stay, Mr. And Mrs. Stanten."

"Thank you."

"Oh no—" I began, but Mr. Stanten held my hands so tightly I wasn't able to utter another word. He then told the person who assisted us another *thank you.*

I was escorted to the elevator. The bellboy followed shortly behind. With Mr. Stanten's hands in mine, pressing tightly, tears of pain ran from my eyes to my cheeks.

"Here we are at 1418," he told the bellboy.

"Yes, sir, I'll get the door."

The nice gentleman opened the door for us to enter and placed our luggage into the bedroom. After he was tipped, the bellboy left us with a smile on his face. The tip was probably worth more than his paycheck. When the door was closed, my hand was released, and I was struck across my face by Mr. Stanten.

"You have no right to touch me like that. I don't care who you are." It angered me for him to think that he had the right to do what he wanted when he wanted.

"As vice president of this company, things are going to be done my way, so if I tell you to do something, I'll expect you to do just that."

"Then I quit." Wow, I finally said it.

"You didn't catch sight of the big picture, Daphina. Now since I have been promoted to vice president of the company, I will make sure that you'll never exercise your advertising abilities in any company. Since quitting is not an option, you don't have to concern yourself about unemployment. So I'll demand you to sit, to stand, to talk, to walk, or even lay with me. You'll be my personal assistant, and, oh, dump that boyfriend of yours. Oh yes, word got out. I don't think you would want him to lose his job, would you? By the way, you're sleeping on the sofa tonight. The sight of you is sickening to me."

The bedroom door slammed behind him. For twenty minutes, I stood in that very same spot. I was stunned about what had just happened. I was blinded by my own tears and needed someone to confide in.

The night fell upon the city of Washington, DC. I sat on the sofa, still clothed in my travel clothes and hungry. It was later that night when there was a knock on the door.

"Room service."

Apparently Mr. Stanten ordered food for us. I opened the door and tipped him with the money I had. Mr. Stanten opened the door to the bedroom and ordered me to bring the food in. I did what was ordered and left.

"I didn't ask you to leave," he said. I'd returned to the bedroom. I knew what was required from me. After the meal, my nightmare was my reality.

The next day, we met with up the people who required our services. Mr. Stanten spoke highly of me, and the clients were itching to get started. After four hours, the clients loved what they had encountered. Some of my best work was presented that day. I was impressed myself. Maybe I carried the fear in my heart and the anxiety in being on a short leash. I only knew failure was not an option.

One more day stood in the way of our departure from Washington, DC. My new vice president of a boss wanted to finalize everything the very next day, but it was that night when the clients wanted to celebrate the working progress on their project. Mr. Stanten and I were taken out to an extravagant restaurant. The night went well. Being around other people had me relaxed a bit more. Well, Mr. Stanten had his dinner, and behind the closed door of the hotel room, he had his dessert.

On our final day, we met with the clients for the last time. I made sure that I continued to restrain my posture and facial expressions to a professional level. It was, after all, my predicament I had with Mr. Stanten. Dragging strangers into my dilemma would be messy and dangerous.

It was two o'clock in the afternoon, and the job was done. The next step, we were traveling home. Our bags were packed, and the room was paid in full. The limo was resting outside the hotel, waiting for the passengers' arrival. I walked briskly to the limo. The door was opened by the driver. He looked at us and smiled.

Halfway to the limo, Mr. Stanten stopped me. "If you breathe a word of this to anyone, I'll make sure you'll regret every word. Do you understand?"

"I'm afraid I do." Fear paralyzed me. I remained flabbergasted during the entire trip, and Mr. Stanten did me the favor of replicating the same behavior on our trip to Washington, DC: voiceless.

Back in the city of San Francisco, I was dropped off at work. I immediately rushed to my car and threw my bags into the trunk. I drove off quickly, but not suspiciously. I went home and cried. I was lost and alone. I spent my Thursday and Friday at home. I needed to weigh out my options, but the unthinkable occurred during my thoughts and developed into a reality.

T-Zone Advertising Inc. called and rejected my attempt for future employment, and if the day couldn't get any worse, Sieta Inc. called and thanked me for my interest, but they were not open for new hires. I was then waiting for the Oracle.

It was Friday night. I couldn't restrain myself from crying. With a bottle of tequila in my hand, I was going to drink myself to sleep. My drinking into unconsciousness was interrupted by a phone call. To my surprise, it was Stephanie.

"Hey, Daphina, I hope I not disturbing you."

"Oh no, please, I'm glad you called," I lied.

"Are you busy? If you're not, I know a place where we can have a late dinner. Daphina, we need to talk."

Before hanging up, we set a time to meet. Boy, I was looking forward to getting drunk. It was seven-thirty at night. A little after eight o'clock, Stephanie and I met up at the UNO pizza restaurant. The place was jumping on a Friday night. Stephanie and I managed to sit at a booth in the corner of the restaurant. The order was taken, and we were ready to talk.

"Stephanie, this is an interesting place to talk. It's pretty rowdy."

"I cannot take the risk of someone hearing us."

"What is all the cloak and dagger?"

"Daphina, if you know what's good for you, you'll leave the company."

I began to express my concerns, but she wanted me to take heed.

"Listen please, I know. I got pregnant with James's baby but refused to abort it. After the baby was born, the person you call Mr. Stanten couldn't risk having me work too close to him. People at the office may be slow, but they carry the common sense God has given them to put the pieces of the puzzle together. So I became the receptionist. He threatens me if I say I'm leaving the company. The thing was, he wanted to keep close tabs on me. I cannot afford to be unemployed, and his threat was upholding any future employment with someone else. He doesn't pay for child support, so I'm on my own. I'm not able to converse to anyone about my mishap, not even the police. Before you came along, he would ask, or should I say demand, for me to stay after hours. It was his way to satisfy his sweet tooth before going home to his wife. He has a thing for younger women, an addiction you may say. He's a kind of man to take what he wants, and at this point, he never suffers the consequence in his violations to women. It was the first time and couple of other occasions, when I refused and fought back, he took from me what he wanted, leaving behind bruises as souvenirs. But I have a confession to make. I was grateful that James had someone else to violate."

I couldn't believe my ears. Did I hear her correctly?

"I know what you must be thinking about me. I have a three-year-old son who sees his mommy cry when she comes home. Daphina, James still comes to me. Well, until three months ago. I could tell when you pissed him off. I feel like a ragdoll without a voice. I want out, but I can't do it alone. He has become more and more violent."

"Stephanie, I had no idea, but I'm not the person to help you." I explained my story and the experience I had to endure during my business trip.

The pizza arrived to our table, but neither of us was able to eat.

"I believe in Mr. Stanten's threats, and because he is vice president of the company, my choices in life are very limited. I had to break off my relationship with Richard. He was more concerned about me than our separation. In his mind, our relationship is still kindled, but I'm afraid for him in losing his job."

"I'm getting the sense that you have not told him the reason for the break up."

"Are you crazy?" I snapped.

"Forgive me in what I'm about to say, but you have brought this upon yourself."

"Excuse me?"

"Daphina, you had a choice to sleep with him or remain a mail distributor, but you have chosen to sleep with him to gain a title for yourself. I didn't have that choice. Now you're trapped in a predicament that you're not able to escape from. I have to know, was it worth it?"

"You know, I have a few choice words that would set you back hundred feet, but I can't, because you're right. I had an alternative, but at that time I preferred to sleep with the devil to get what I wanted, and now I'm paying the consequences."

"I believe God is going to make a way."

"I don't believe in God."

"Maybe you should. I gave my life to Christ last year. It was then that James stopped coming after me. I chastised him in the name of Jesus, of course, and he would flee, just like the devil. His threats didn't expire, but his time with me has. It's time for you to get yourself to Christ, and in time I believe that he will free us from this mess."

"Thank you, Stephanie, but not now."

"We will get through this together."

The night continued on, and neither of us had the solution to our problems. Well, for her it was Jesus Christ, but the reality stood, and we couldn't withstand the possibility of becoming homeless. If we decided to quit and run, our fate would unravel into something horrific.

The plot in shredding James Stanten with his dignity was brought to an end. The entire weekend was reserved in what could be done, but without a higher power on our side, the days would go on as intended.

Monday morning came bright and new. As cold as it was, I made sure I was concealed in warmth. Traveling to work, I was summing up my self-worth. I wasn't able to accumulate a tally beyond zero.

On the fifteenth floor in the workplace, I glanced around every cubicle for Mr. Stanten, but the coworkers were giving me an inscrutable look. It was then I entered my office to find the answer. I left the door ajar, but somehow the door found its way to connect with the door frame. Startled, I quickly turned around to discover Mr. Stanten leaning against the wall near my emergency exit.

I dropped everything I had onto the floor. He bellowed and disputed about my job-seeking moments. He wasn't able to lash out his terrorization, but he made it known that he was liable for the job rejections.

"In my office," he said. His office was in a secluded place; voices were not able to filter into the wrong pair of ears. "I'm going to lay down some ground rules." But once again, I knew what he wanted. He wanted to prove that he was still in control. The door was closed; he gave a stare of intimidation. The veins on his neck were in plain sight. His skin was flushed, and his anger surfaced. The rules were in place, and there was nothing left to say. He stormed out, leaving the door wide open for the executives to observe. For once in my life, the fortitude I had to flee from the prison that I've built from myself was burning within my belly, but it's just knowing how to get it out.

Closing hours stirred around, and I made my way to the office of Satan. People were still lingering around, catching up on a few things. Making sure my appearance remained in good spirits was a task. Mr. Stanten wasn't sitting at his desk but rather leaning on front of his desk. "So what took you?" he starts off. I stood by the door in fear, still reminded of the incident earlier that day. "You know the drill, come." I approached him, and the anger surfaced and the rage was unleashed. Rape was his pleasure that night; his strength maxed out his disciplined. With his hand clutched to my neck, it was that night he warned me about the consequences in turning against him. When I was released, I ran out of the office into mine. Running from my office, I ran into Richard.

"Daphina, where are you going? We really need to talk." I didn't want to talk. The more I fidgeted in the vicinity of his presence, the more reason he wanted to stop me. "Something is wrong, isn't it, Daphina? Just talk to me!" I was startled with the elevation of his voice, still timid in the past occurrence.

"Do you love your job, Richard?"

"Yes, of course, why?"

"Do you love me?"

"Is this a joke? Yes, I wish I could tell you a million times."

"Then you should mind your business."

"Daphina, wait!" I grew a deaf ear and rushed out. Drowning in my misery, I wanted to die. I walked swiftly into the night air for ventilation, but it was raining. I was standing outside in a pool of shame, laced with disgrace, but most of all, the resentment I detained against the company. I stood in the midst of the rain, watching my clothes getting damp, damper, and then soaked. I not once grumbled about my current circumstances, I just stood in front of my job, watching this old woman sympathizing for me. I thought she was a wicked woman who wouldn't mind her business, but it was I who was wicked and now depressed.

It was later in the evening, and I wanted to withdraw myself from this and into the comfort of my own home. I approached the doors to Devine for Design, my job and my curse. I've noticed that I had my purse strapped around my shoulder, dangling and wet. With the exception of my jacket, I had everything I needed. I turned around to start my journey home. I left my car resting in its parking space and walked. It was ten miles to the Westlake Village Apartments. I took off my three inch heels and continued to distance myself from the job. With my feet bare, wet and cold, my controllable strength carried me. From the corner of my eye, I thought I saw the old woman following me, but without an umbrella shielding my body, the darkness and the rain blinded my sight.

"For what profit it is to a man," the woman yelled, "if he gains the whole world and loses his own soul?"

"Shut up, old woman. I know now."

I started to run, but my feet felt like they were frozen, and the weight was unbearable, but somehow I was running. I looked back to see if she was following close behind. She stood there in place and expressed amusement. I continued to run with my bare feet until I reached the Muni bus stop. I sat and rested.

"James, rest his soul, described, 'Each person is tempted when he is drawn away and enticed by his own evil desires,'" the old woman said.

The old woman stood on the opposite side of me with her umbrella over her head, smiling. The bus picked her up. She carried an angry look on her face as the bus drove off. *She's right*, I thought, *and I was wrong*. I didn't have to agree with the indecent proposal, but then again, the thought was already brought to my attention by someone else. I wished I stopped the affair long ago. I could have at any time, but at this stage of the game, it was all over for me. The bus arrived and took me to my destination. I no longer had the ability to walk. Once again, I scalded my flesh to remove any memory of his touch, but who's going to remove the memory I had in my mind? I still remember the verbal contract I had with Mr. Stanten. I began to torment myself with that decision. My actions weren't any better than my sister's.

I went back to work like nothing had happened. Richard couldn't help himself; he started to approach me, but I held up my hand to stop him. I turned myself from him and walked into my office. I locked the door, dropped my things, and began to work. Approximately twenty minutes into my workday, I received a phone call.

"Hello, Daphina."

"Yes."

"This is Victoria from The Oracle Enterprise. We received your résumé, and the president of the company would like to interview you tomorrow at noon. Are you still interested?"

I paused for a second or two. "Yes, I'm sorry, I was taken by surprise."

"That's okay. So I'll see you tomorrow."

"I have to speak with Mr. Stanten to leave early."

"Oh, that will not be a problem. James is scheduled for a business meeting first thing tomorrow morning. It is recommended for you to be present at this interview on time. It is also required to dress comfortably. We will need about two hours of your time."

"Well, Victoria, if it is not going to be a problem with my boss, I'll be there tomorrow."

"Good. I'll announce to the president that you're coming. See you tomorrow, Daphina."

"Yes, thank you."

In the midst of my storm, I was given a little touch of life. I know this interview will carry out well. It has to. No one would question my coming in late from lunch on the day of the interview, so that would deal with the office snitch. Now I was counting the hours of the day. Work didn't seem to have any significance. My future latitude was my new attitude.

Wednesday morning was delivered on a silver platter. I had on my best attire. I wanted that job. The night before, I brought work home to catch up and stand ahead of any surprises that may occur in my absence. At work, I was pleased that I didn't have anything to do. Well, it wasn't until Mr. Stanten displayed himself in my office. The sight of him sickened me, but what made matters worse was he wanted to perform a physical meeting. Right away, my joyful spirit was shadowed by his wicked means. Again, I wanted to die under his care.

Getting dressed, Mr. Stanten said, "I'm leaving today on a business trip. I need some ideas on an ad." He opened the door and continued, "This is all the information that you'll need to be creative." In front of the office, he handed me the paperwork. "I'll check on your progress tomorrow."

How clever, I thought, keeping people guessing on the true nature of his visit. Behind closed doors there were many secrets. I wanted death to come for those who know. My thoughts were defective, and I needed to end it. Mr. Stanten left the office, and I got to work. After ten o'clock, I found myself glancing at my watch every so often until eleven-thirty. At that time it was time to leave, my future lies ahead. While walking to the elevator, Richard approached me.

"So where are you headed?"

"Do you mind joining me for a ride to the lobby?"

"Yes, why not?"

There were two elevators stationed next to each other and while waiting for one of them to open, more people gathered to use it. One elevator door opened and so did the other.

"Can you guys use the other elevator?" I asked them. Without care, they used the other elevator, and Richard and I began to talk.

"I missed you, Richard, and in time we will talk, but now I'm headed to a meeting."

"You look pretty chipper today, and since when do you attend a meeting without Mr. Stanten? You're looking for a new job, are you?"

"Richard, this is the time that I really need for you to be quiet, please."

The doors opened to the elevator. "When you find what you're looking for, don't forget to send me an invite."

I smiled on the way to the door, but at the same time, I've noticed that Stephanie wasn't at her post. "Excuse me, where is Stephanie?"

"Oh, you must be talking about the person who used to work here. She quit yesterday. My name is Roxanne, and I'm taking her place. What's your name?"

"Daphina," I said a little distraught.

"Nice to meet you."

"Thanks, for the information, Roxanne. I'll see you when I come back." I rushed to my car. I was now a little behind schedule.

Hastening in and out of traffic, I made it to The Oracle on time. The craftsmanship of the building was breathtaking, but when I made my way into the building, it felt like I was entering into the twenty-second century. I couldn't get enough of someone's artistic design. "Hello," someone said, approaching me. "You must be Daphina. We have been expecting you."

"Who are you?"

"I'm sorry, let me formally introduce myself. My name is Evelina Scott. I'm the secretary for the president of this company. If you don't mind, I need you to follow me to her office."

"The president is a woman?"

"You're looking for a male president?" She laughed. "Daphina, we get a lot of people with the same expectation."

I was relieved, but couldn't help but to crack a smile. We talked about the company and the expectations for about five minutes.

"So Evelina, where is the president? I'm beginning to think that she's a myth."

"Okay, that is funny, but let me ensure you that she's not a myth. The president has four different offices, and today she is located on the top floor in an exclusive area.

You'll see; we're almost there. You're probably wondering why she has four different offices in one building."

"Yes, as a matter of fact."

"The answer is simple. The Oracle is so capacious, traveling to her office can be a little challenging. So wherever she is in the building, she'll have an office close by."

"Fair enough."

"That was my thought exactly." The workout was great, but the interview was far greater than life itself, and I wanted it all to begin. "Well, here we are. Let me buzz her and see if she's ready for you. Feel free to look around."

On the thirty-fourth floor, this level was decked out for the president's interest only. I couldn't see anyone else around. The décor was exotic but in good taste. This place was a vision. Beautiful plants, waterfall, chairs, stone tiles, books, skylight, leather seating, maps, future plans of something, collectible items—

"Stop drooling, Daphina," Evelina said. "The president is ready to see you now." It was twelve-sixteen in the afternoon, and I was very optimistic about this interview. I can already taste the sign of victory. Evelina opened the door and announced my presence. "Mrs. Stanten, your appointment has arrived. Good luck, Daphina."

She closed the door behind me, and my heart just stopped.

"Hello Daphina, it's good to see you again. If you don't mind, I rather if you didn't take a seat."

What the...

"You're joining me to my home for lunch. If you will, follow me. The company car is waiting."

Okay, Daphina, breathe.

"This is not necessary, Mrs. Stanten. I don't want you to put yourself out because I work for your husband."

"What gives you the notion that I'm doing this for you?"

Oh my, I messed up.

"I'm sorry. I didn't mean to misinterpret your actions."

"Enjoy the ride, dear. We have much to talk about."

I hope she meant that in a positive way.

The ride was lengthy, but her home was massive and brilliantly crafted. I didn't know how to take on her invitation into her private Chabot. There I was resting my eyes on the beautiful Spanish/Mediterranean home on Moulin in Tiburon, California. We had lunch on the terrace, and shortly after I was escorted to the library.

"Thank you for lunch, Mrs. Stanten."

"A thank you is not necessary. It was my pleasure. Now let's get down to business, shall we. I think I've taken enough of your time. I remember your interest in my company some time ago, but when you were called for an interview, you had already taken your rightful position at Devine for Design, hum? So what is your interest in my company now?"

She was going to call. I wished I had known that before because I wouldn't be in the predicament I was in now. I wanted to say, oh, you're a female and I'll be respected as a person with an incredible work tactic and not for my body.

"Why the sudden change of employment?" she asked.

I didn't know how to respond to the question, so I enlightened her about the discrimination I had experienced during my days of employment but didn't elaborate. She noted in what had been said but didn't comment on it. She leaned back in her chair after sitting up for almost an hour, but when she leaned back, I noticed something familiar lying next to her.

She asked another question. "To what extent would you take to climb the ladder in a corporation?"

"Hard work," I told her. I explained my accomplishments and gave her proof of satisfactory letters from clients. After viewing the letters, I could tell that she was intrigued. I was curious about something Mrs. Stanten said earlier, but it couldn't be.

In the midst of another thought, she asked another question. "What are your thoughts on your current employer?"

She was the wicked woman and knew right away that the clothing lying next to her reminded me of someone.

"You're the old woman? Please be honest with me."

"It wasn't my intention to fabricate any information from you. I wanted for you to know."

"So why all that get up? Why did you just come to me?"

"The question I should be asking is why didn't you come to me? I thought at first that you were a floozy that would stop at nothing to explore in the world of riches, but I was wrong. You were haunted by the words of God because I wanted you to stop sleeping with my husband."

"You knew?"

"Darling, in my age, ignorance doesn't knock at my doorstep. I knew. Women would flaunt themselves to him at times, and in my presence, but none of this ever took place at his workplace. They feared him. Your friend Stephanie came to The Oracle, explaining and exploiting everything. So you see, Daphina, when my assistant presented me a list of potential candidates for an upcoming position, I was amazed to see your name, and I knew Stephanie's anecdote was disturbing but authentic."

"Where is Stephanie now, and what are you going to do with this information?"

"Stephanie didn't leave her return address or number. I believe that she may be on the run. Speaking on what I'm going to do with this info, well, that is a question for you. I am, by the way, hiring you. In order to work for me, you have to sever off some bad piece of luggage." She leaned toward me and said, "As a woman, I know you have a way in getting back and hard. Get your people you can trust—"

I interrupted her. "Are you going to sweet talk the media with a story?"

"Darling, I knew there was something about you I liked."

We continued to converse, and I remained conscious to the fact that I was in her territory. I told her everything on the subject of the secret behind closed doors. Mrs. Stanten was on the edge of her seat, feeling disgusted and betrayed. I glanced at my phone, anxious that Mr. Stanten would call, but Mrs. Staten knew what was going on and assured me that he would be occupied with meetings all day with her blessings. More than two hours were consumed, and I was feeling a little unnerved.

"Why are you fidgeting? You work for me now. When you return, drop off your resignation letter to the president. I'm sure you have a hard copy at your disposal."

I smiled and began to relax.

After three o'clock, I was escorted to the limo. The journey began once again, but this time we were returning back to her office. It was about twenty minutes when Mrs. Stanten cleared her throat and said, "Are you a Christian?"

"No. Why?"

"It's unsettling that a bright young woman would give up access to her body as an exchange for success."

"Sometimes you have to do something you don't agree in order to survive."

"Do you mind?"

"Not at all."

She opened her Bible and said, "This Holy Bible is in an English Version. I'm reading this for you to understand. In James 4:1, it begins, 'Why do you fight and argue with each other? Isn't it because you are full of selfish desires that fight to control your body? You want something you don't have, and you will do anything to get it. You will even kill! But you still cannot get what you want, and you won't get it by fighting and arguing. You should pray for it. Yet even when you do pray, your prayers are not answered, because you pray just for self-reasons. You people aren't faithful to God! Don't you know that if you love the world, you are God's enemy? And if you decide to be a friend of the world, you make yourself an enemy of God.' Do you doubt the Scripture that says, 'God truly cares about the spirit he has put in us'? In fact, God treats us with even greater kindness, just as the Scripture says, 'God opposes everyone who is proud, but He is kind to everyone who is humble. Surrender to God! Resist the devil, and he will run from you. Draw near to God, and he will draw near to you. Clean up your lives, you sinners. Purify your hearts, you people who can't make up your mind.'"

"Please stop," I said. "I have to say that this is heavy material. How did you do that?"

"And what would that be?"

"How is it that you're finding something that pertains to me?"

"Everything we need to know and learn is in this book."

"What does it mean when you love the world? You're God's enemy?"

"Well, Christians live in the world, but they're not of it. This world consists of adultery, gays, fornicators, drug abusers, murderers, thieves—"

"I get it. The world is infested with people practicing sin."

"Right, Daphina. Listen to me, I'm not pushing the Word of God on you. This will be yours to decide."

"I don't mind, Mrs. Stanten. Someway, somehow, the Word is comforting to me. I've lived in the world, and it has provided me with sadness and despair."

"We have made it back to the company now. This is my personal cell number. Please do not hesitate to use it. Build a case against my husband. Make sure you file for sexual harassment and turn in a letter of resignation. See who is willing to assist you in making some of this happen. I'll keep in touch." I was making my way out of the limo when she said, "Daphina, start looking for another place to stay. You may want to relocate. If he is as dangerous as you say he is, relocating is your best option. As a matter of fact, I do suggest for you to do so."

"Yes, I will. I'll get started on it."

"Daphina," she called again, "find a reasonable place to live. I'll get you an advance on your paycheck. A home or condo is what you seek. Take it. Your position in my company will pay you enough to keep up the mortgage and property taxes and other bills you may have."

"Mrs. Stanten, I cannot ask for you to do this."

"You didn't. Get to work, Daphina. Tootles."

I walked to my car. I was happy, sad, scared, but most of all, I was born again. I went to work and made a quick visit to human resources and filed for sexual harassment. It was then that I traveled to my office to retrieve my letter of resignation to take to effect in a couple of weeks.

The president made himself available to meet. I told him I would only take a few minutes of his time. When I arrived into his office, I placed my resignation into his hand, but not one word was spoken. He accepted the letter, and he spoke to me to wish me luck. I hesitated a little when leaving his office. His facial gestures were disfigured, and I needed to know why.

"Mr. Colter, are you at least interested in why I'm leaving the company?" I asked.

"No, I'm just relieved that you're moving on. We don't need whores in this business."

"Excuse me."

"Yes, you're excused, and if you don't mind, you can—"

"Mr. Colter, with all due respect, if Mr. Stanten is feeding you with exotic food and wine to twist your perception of me, the truth will soon find you. I feel sorry for you as the president of this company and not knowing what is going on under your nose. As pigs as you are, you and Mr. Stanten can go to your natural habitat and wallow in the same mud for all I care!" I walked off and didn't respond to his remarks. I think he was trying to apologize, but who needed it?

I returned gracefully to my office, and Richard ran up from behind.

"Daphina, Mr. Stanten has been calling everyone here to find you. He seems upset that you're leaving."

"Oh good. I don't know how he found out so quickly, but you don't have to worry yourself about anything."

"But wait, how can I not worry about something I don't know anything about?"

"Richard, there are many things I kept secret from you and many I'm not proud of. If it is not any trouble, do you mind having dinner with me? I'll explain everything, I promise. By then, if you don't want to have me as a girlfriend, I'll understand."

"Riddle me this, riddle me that, I don't like riddles. Just tell me now."

"I can't now. You'll understand. Listen, it's four-eleven now, can we have dinner at seven?"

"No, let's try for six o'clock. We can meet up at our usual, private place."

"Scomas's?"

"Right, try giving Mr. Stanten a call. He seemed upset."

"Like I care. See you at six."

I watched him walk away. His face was dressed with worries, but I was relieved to finally have a chance to expose Mr. Stanten to him and hopefully to the world. Back to my office, I gave Mr. Stanten a call. Every other word was filled with profanity and threats. He was ending his business trip short to show up here first thing in the morning. I had a little time to make business calls. When he was finished addressing me with filthy names, I hung up the phone. I sat in my chair contemplating, my next move, and somehow

Whanda came to mind. Down to the basement, oh, I remembered it all too well. I didn't waste time.

"Whanda," I called unprofessionally across the room. She was slaving at her workplace as usual.

"Let's go to the office," she suggested. "Now what's going on that couldn't wait?"

"I need to know how I can locate Stephanie, our previous receptionist."

"I know who she is, but I cannot help you."

"I'm planning on exposing Mr. Stanten to the media, and I need help."

"Daphina, Mr. Stanten is a powerful man. He is no one to play around with. If you're seriously going to fight, you're going to have fight all the way if you want to win. I'll call Stephanie myself. You both should have come to me about this in the first place. I've seen his affairs, but I didn't know he was sadistic."

"She told you about me?"

"Yes, it was my idea to bring this up with his wife. I'll help you with everything you need. Call me. Here is my number."

Hugging Whanda, I said, "Thank you."

She neglected her duties and carried on an extensive conversation, but in the midst of it, my parents traveled to my thoughts. I didn't want to caution them of the things to come, but I knew I had to.

"Whanda, I have to leave. I have a dinner date in a half an hour, and I have to notify my family in what had been going on."

"Why did you wait this long, Daphina?"

"Shame. Whanda, it was out of shame. I'll see you later."

I was out the door and running to my car when Richard called. "Yes, I'm on my way. I'm standing next to my car. You're already there. Okay, that's good idea to reserve a spot. I'll see you in twenty minutes. Okay, I love you too. Bye."

With the key in the door, trying to open it in a hurry, I felt a weight pushing me onto the window of my car. Losing all control of my body, I fell back and onto the ground. I saw Mr. Stanten looking over me, saying, "No one leaves me, no one! Your friend Stephanie should have been your example of that."

He rambled on, but I blacked out.

Waking up was hard to do. I was finally conscious to the pain. I gathered that it was the next day. The sun illuminated through the window of my private room in the hospital. I noticed that the doctor was speaking with someone whose back was turned against me.

"It seems that someone is awake," the doctor said, while approaching me. "So, besides the pain, how are you doing?"

"I wouldn't know," I began, "since the pain is dominating everything."

"Perhaps that wasn't the brightest question to ask," he smiled and sat next to the hospital bed. "I want to keep you for another day. You have a slight concussion and a fractured wrist. I'll have a nurse to take your vitals. You have any questions for me?"

"No, well, yes. Who brought me here?"

"You have your boyfriend to thank. I'll be back to check up on you at the end of my shift. I'll leave you two alone."

"Thank you, Doctor."

Richard, now leaning on the edge of the bed, smiled in relief.

"How did you find me?"

"After waiting at the restaurant for almost an hour and you not answering your cell, I knew something was wrong. So I searched the job, but everyone remembered you leaving. I tried the parking lot, and well, I saw you lying there bloody and unconscious, so I dialed 911. And here you are."

I smiled at him, and he sat closer to me. I stroked his cheek. I was pleased that he was my knight and shining armor. Well, the moment was there until he asked, "Are you aware at all in who is responsible for this?"

"If I told you, you wouldn't believe me."

"Try me."

"Mr. Stanten."

He looked at me and said, "You're right, I don't believe you."

I explained everything from the very beginning. He didn't take it well. Who would? But he continued to listen until I was finished.

"That explains why you broke up with me and your unnerving behavior. I wish you had trusted me with this from the beginning. I have family who are able to help you."

"I'm sorry Richard, your family comes from a Christian background, and as you may not know, I'm not a Christian."

"Have I once judged you?"

"No."

"Have I turned my back on you or push my faith on you?"

"No."

"Have I always been there for you?"

"Yes."

"So what's the trouble? I love you, but you have to learn to love yourself."

"I feel filthy and unworthy of you and God's love."

"Do you want to become a child of God?"

"Yes, but—"

"I don't want to hear 'but.' Take charge of your life by giving it to God. Say the repentance prayer with me."

"Okay."

The prayer was gentle and comforting. I was giving all my dirty laundry to God. For once in my life, I was at peace. After accepting Christ as my Lord and Savior, a couple of officers came into my room with a cup of coffee in their midst.

"Hello, Ms. Chavez. My name is Detective Will Rizzo, and this is Detective Nick Manek. We're here to get a statement from you."

I wasn't in the mood, but I gave my statement. I didn't stop there. Detective Manek asked more questions about Mr. Stanten. I told as much as I could, but I suggested for them to speak with Stephanie Malone.

"She's not going to speak with us," Detective Manek alleged.

"Why is that?"

"Her attacker placed her in a coma and has been that way for three days. Witnesses gave James Stanten's description, but we're not able to locate him."

"I have nothing else to offer you two detectives."

"We're getting the notion that he has become dangerous and recommend that you should stay with someone until he is captured."

"You can stay with me," Richard offered.

"Are you sure?"

"I wouldn't offer if I wasn't sure." He smiled.

"All right." Detective Rizzo understood. "We'll be in touch."

As they were leaving the room, I made a remark to Richard. "This occurrence feels like one of your typical suspense/drama movies, but this one so happens to be real."

The night pursued on to the light of day, and with noticed, I was released from the hospitals care. A few bumps and bruises and I was set free. Richard drove me to his home, and what a home. I was able to freshen up before returning to work to collect all my belongings. For the last time, I was airlifted to the fifteenth floor. It was the middle of the day, and the employees stopped what they were doing and fastened their optical vision onto me. Somehow my incident found its way to the media, and now everyone knew.

"Ignore them," Richard responded. "Let's go to your office and gather your possessions."

In the office, I gathered everything that didn't belong to the company. I called all the ongoing clients in the regards of their projects. I began to suggest Richard as a replacement. Richard waved his hands vigorously to get my attention.

"I'm leaving, too," he whispered. Digging deep into the soil of mother earth, I retrieved one of my old ways. I've given the new clients the name of the president without revealing his title and announced that he was taking over. I also made sure they were given his private line. My job was done.

"Well, we have everything packed. What now?" I wondered.

"The cars are loaded with our things, so if you want, you can follow me back to my place."

"I need to get some of my clothes, toothbrush, and toothpaste—you know, stuff."

He held up his hands. "Okay, I got it." He followed me home.

"I'll only be a moment. You can wait here."

"I don't think so. I'm coming in." He searched the apartment for any surprises and began to assist me with my packing. Having him there sped up the process.

After loading half of my apartment into my car, I tailed Richard back to his home. In his home, I was given a grand tour. "And this is your room. All the drawers belong to you, so you can unpack now if you like. I'll be downstairs preparing dinner."

"And you cook too."

"If you're interested, you can have the full package."

I couldn't help it, I had to laugh. *How did I get so lucky?*

"Daphina, if you need anything, I'll be downstairs."

"Okay, thanks."

A man like that, hum. I really made a mess of things, but he stood right there. God is real, and to have someone like Richard, well, if you said *blessed*, you must have read my mind. I sat on the edge of my queen-sized bed in a king-sized room as my thoughts became clear to me. Looking over my life, I had long established that I had become my sister. She gave her body for attention as I gave mine for success. Whatever it took, right? I didn't believe in God. Why should I worship someone I have never seen but, with my lack of observation, sheltered the truth? My own mother made the commitment to give up her life to the Lord. Her whole disposition had changed, and her sweet spirit perfumed her existence. Through her, God's existence was no longer a myth. The world cannot replicate the Spirit of God if they tried. The true nature of the beast would eventually reveal itself. One cannot hide who they really are.

"Daphina," Richard said out of breath. "You didn't get very far with your unpacking."

Drained from my thoughts, I was slow to answer.

"Daphina, are you feeling okay?"

"Yes, just trying to figure out why you're so out of breath. You weren't doing laps around the kitchen?"

"Oh, how did you know?"

"Funny, well, let us go. I'm ready to experience your concoction."

From that moment on, I felt secured. For approximately three days, we were roommates. Mr. Stanten didn't make himself accessible for the authorities to find him, so they searched and sustained to find new leads. In the meantime, I wasn't able to attend my new job or any long joyrides, so grocery shopping was my insanity breaker. With Richard working at his new job, I needed something to do. Riley's Food Market was eight minutes away, and I had an immediate urge to mingle around people, even though it was at the grocery store. I was tailed by an unmarked police car to the market. Driving down each aisle in Riley's with my shopping basket, I grabbed everything that tickled my interest. Making a turn into another aisle, someone whispered my name. I wasn't going to be the victim you would see in a horror flick when curiosity expires their life. I continued to push my overweight basket, speaking to customers as they passed. The interest grew when the reluctant, overweight basket refused to turn onto the pasta aisle. The basket was full, and the steering was impossible. Squatting down to the floor to make my selection of particular pasta, my name was called again, but at a closer range. I could feel the breath, breathing down my neck. *Okay, Daphina, this is not a horror flick film. This is real life, girl. Get a grip.* I stood up slowly and made a 180 degree turn. My fear manifested into something horrifying: Mr. Stanten. He stood close and revealed his armor tucked away on his left side of his trousers.

"Is that supposed to scare me?" I said bravely.

"If you don't want anyone harmed here today, you'll follow my instructions."

Without any further ado, I followed his instructions into the back of the store, neglecting my basket full of goods. At the loading dock, we encountered the workers bickering and complaining. I was grabbed by the arm, and we fled the scene. In the alley, Mr. Stanten took out his pistol, a healthy .457 magnum. He used the front end of the gun to push down my blouse.

"You've got to be kidding."

"The foreplay would be refreshing, and one last dip into the pool for old time sake would fill my spirit with fatness."

"You have no shame," I said with disgust. "You have a wife, riches, and yet you still do the things that are not right. Why lose everything for a piece of flesh?"

He forced me back into the alley where darkness ruled.

"Take it off," he demanded. "Don't worry. You'll have no use for it after I'm done with you. My true attentions are to humiliate you, just as you done to me. My face and my wrong doings are plastered on every newspaper and into every home that is turned on to the six o'clock news. You ended my life, and now I'll end yours. My dark, sleek magnum will end it all for you. You have anything to say?"

"Say what, Mr. Stanten? Do you want me to say, 'Early will I seek you; my soul thirst for you; my flesh longs for you in a dry and thirsty land where there is no water. So I have looked for you in the sanctuary, to see your power and your glory. Because your loving kindness is better than life, my lips shall praise you thus I will bless you while I live; I will lift my hands in your name. My soul shall be satisfied as with marrow and fatness, and my mouth shall praise you with joyful lips. When I remember you on my bed, I meditate on you in the night watches. Because you have been my help, therefore in the shadow of your wings I will rejoice. My soul follows close behind you; your right hand upholds me'? I've changed my life, Mr. Stanten. The first verse of Psalm 63:1 displays, 'O God, you are my God.' You don't own me or my body. I found my Savior who doesn't require me to sin. If you thirst for my body, you'll have to take it because I'm not giving it up anymore. You may take my body, but you cannot take my spirit."

I stood naked and proud, for God had given me a gift to lift my spirit to a climax beyond everyone's reach.

"Bravo, bravo, you found God. Today, I announce that you'll return to your God, naked, beaten, and then killed.

When you first approached me, your beauty corrupted me, and your flesh destroyed me. I'm returning the favor."

I was quickly struck on my lower abdominal and then on the side of my chin. Falling to the ground, he landed on his knees while I was fixated on the pain. I felt all the anger, hatred, and frustration pounding against me, as I was beaten on every inch of my body. He stood back on his feet while I was lying on the ground, bloody and bruised. His revolver clicked in place and his aim was positioned. I continued to pray. I didn't know if God was calling me home or if He wanted me to stay. Either way, I was ready. A black soul like me was purified through my sincerity of my cry of repentance. I no longer feared death but felt joy. Mr. Stanten fired his gun; the bullet traveled to my outer thigh and then the other. He was torching me. I cried out on every impact. He continued with my upper and lower arm. When he was done, he walked toward me and lowered his body and his face. He kissed my bloody lips as I was pulling away.

I was not able to move, and Mr. Stanten pressed his revolver against my chest and smiled. My eye's rested on his, and I said, "I forgive you." A shot was fired and darkness filled his eyes.

"Ms. Chavez, are you all right?" the officer said. He was the one who was assigned to protect me and the very one who tailed me to the super market. With sympathy, he peeled off his jacket and covered me. I guess God wanted me to stay. I didn't mind. As a new Christian, I have a story, a life-changing story. The officer kept me conscious until help arrived, but for the time being, cops swarmed the area, making it their own. My eyes were placed to rest when the sirens were fired up and the speed was accelerated in numbers. What a day.

I woke up one Saturday morning with an agenda. The morning sun radiated my bedroom. It has been five months since my close encounter. Mrs. Stanten did what was promised. The man I thought was deceased was alive and behind prison walls. I cannot be acrimonious; God, after all, is giving Mr. Stanten a chance to become a child of God. I hope he doesn't misuse the time that was given to him. As for me, I woke up in my beautiful, two-story, high-ceiling, green home. The windows in my home are phenomenal. I was relocated to Berkeley, California. Venturing too far from San Francisco was out of the question. I am, after all, working for Mrs. Stanten. So my Seventh Street home was my new citadel, and my prince charming lives in another estate until our wedding day. I had to admit, Mr. Stanten had given me a new life. If it wasn't for him, even though He was always there, God would still be hidden from me. By my hand I would have remained lost in the darkness of Satan's stronghold.

Mr. Stanten's life was spared, but as for Stephanie, she never woke up from her coma. Mrs. Stanten gained custody of Stephanie's son. The court finalized Mr. Stanten's permanent residence in prison. Twenty-five to life, they said. The story of my life.

I am content with my life now. From time to time, I find myself lifting my head to the heavens to whisper a thank you to God. I am able to look into the mirror and like what I see staring back at me. Leaning against the railing of the balcony, I smiled. With the breeze combing through my hair, I was praising God continuously. If it wasn't for Him, I wouldn't be able stand here feeling blessed.

One Month Later...

Life itself has become very busy working for Mrs. Stanten, planning for the wedding, and writing a book. It was shortly after my recovery that a publisher took interest in my story. I didn't know the seriousness of their interest until I received a check in my name. It was a year later when I was resting my back against the chair at my work desk of my home; I was finalizing my thoughts.

We tend to adapt to the comfort of our surroundings, and some are not taking the responsibility of their circumstances. One would swim in a pool of sin where warmth and enjoyment rules their souls. There is no reason for one to give up in what has been satisfying them for many years. And why should they? The desires of their hearts have been met. Oblivious to the nature of Satan, they would continue to swim, performing back strokes or diving beneath the surface. For all they know, heaven lies on Earth. I hope they will never parish to not know that the clean, warm, and glistening water sabotaged their judgment. Everyone's life has an expiration, but don't allow your time on Earth be wasted living the life of sin. Now the water turns against them, pulling them down beneath the surface; those who had been captured, struggle to reach the surface, but one may not be as successful. Satan has now revealed his deceitful plot, but now it is too late. We have a choice to step out from the pool of sin and dry ourselves with the cloth of salvation. The choice is ours to make. God loves us all and hides nothing. A lighted path is lit for us to follow Him. The directions are given, but are we willing to follow Him?

Being a Christian, there is a big shoe to fill. As we grow under the supervision of Christ, we are able to fill that shoe. We cannot cloth ourselves as Christians and continue to cover the wolverine spirit in sheep skin. God knows His children, so what are we thinking that we can fool God?

Don't superior yourself as gods in church or on public grounds; you'll be wasting your time. Just like those who are unable to wear wool without scratching vigorously for relief, that person would soon peel off the wool clothing with satisfaction. One would say the same thing about a wolf in sheep's clothing. The perpetrator is only able to hide for so long before they're sickened by the fact that they cannot hide any longer. They too are relieved when the sheep clothing is removed and the wicked means are revealed.

The Spirit of God is not cold. The genuine Christian will warm the heart of others. This is because the Spirit of God lies in the vessel of His followers. So on this day, I ask, who are you going to serve?

I convinced myself that I would become a successful career woman. I wanted to shine above the failures of my older sister. Success, riches, and respect were the things I needed to succeed as a woman in a man-dominated world. I was willing to do anything to accomplish just that, but things got out of hand as well as the loss of my dignity. In James 1:14, I was the one who was enticed with success. "But each one is tempted when he is drawn anyway by his own desires and enticed." My body is my temple; I know that now. I lost respect when I was trying to get respect, but now I've learned to respect myself. I regret taking the job from Devine for Design. I didn't know that I would be making a deal with the devil. Discovering that Mrs. Stanten's personnel was going to call me in for an interview was like putting salt onto an injury. I wish I had known.

The message I want revealed is to love and respect yourself. In the moment of the verbal agreement I had with Mr. Stanten, I was selling out for the desires of my heart. But let me tell you, compromising can sometimes create an overwhelming problem. My success became empty because in what I had to do to get there and maintain it. I've learned that the Holy Bible highlights in Ecclesiastes 2:4-11:

> I made my works great; I built myself houses, and planted myself vineyards. I made myself gardens and orchards and I planted all kinds of fruits tree in them. I made myself water pools from which to water the growing trees of the grove. I acquired male and female servants, and had servants born in my house. Yes, I had greater possessions of herds and flocks than all who were in Jerusalem before me. I also gather for myself silver and gold and the special treasures of kings and of the province. I acquired male and female singers, the delight of the sons of men and musical instruments of all kinds. So I became great and excelled more than all who were before me in Jerusalem. Also my wisdom remained with me. Whatever my desired I did not keep from them. I did not withhold my heart from any pleasures. For my heart rejoiced in all my labor; and this was my reward from all my labor. Then I looked all the works that my hands had done and the labor in which I had toiled an indeed all was

vanity and grasping for the wind. There was no profit under the sun.

I sacrificed to get where I needed to be and proved to myself and the executives with the evidence of my work that I was more than able to do my job, but I wasn't fulfilled. I felt empty. God wasn't the answer to my frustrations. I and I alone thought she could do it herself, but I learned in John 15:1-8 when Jesus said,

> I am the true vine, and My Father is the vinedresser. Every branch in Me that does not bear fruit He takes away, and every branch that bears fruit He prunes, that it may bear more fruit. You are already clean because the word which I have spoken to you. Abide in Me, and I in you. As the branch cannot bear fruit of itself, unless it abides in the vine, neither can you, unless you abide in Me. I am the vine, you are the branches. He who abides in Me, and I in him, bears much fruit; for without Me you can do nothing. If anyone does not abide in Me, he is cast out as a branch and is withered; and they gather them and throw them into the fire, and they are burned. If you abide in Me, and My words abide in you, you will ask what you desire, and it shall be done for you. By this My Father is glorified, that you bear much fruit; so you will be My disciples.

I've tried it my way, and I didn't get very far, but when I invited God into my life, I felt that I had a purpose. I became that branch that produced many fruits. We should know that we cannot do things on our own without the help of God. We may try, but why?

A Final Word of Thought

Sasha is back and still on track.

Five years later, I found myself reading Psalm 23, the fourth verse. This scripture struck me off my feet. It leads me back to my past life. Can I acquaint with you the significance of this verse that helped me and perhaps even you?

Counseling men and women in my line of work helped me to grow in Christ even further, and perhaps when I counsel you regarding Psalm 23:4 that it will help you to understand and to grow in Christ as well.

You're probably wondering if things are going well for you, how you can be in darkness. Well, if you're indulging yourself in sinful behavior in this world, you're meander in darkness. The world is polluted with sin, and its impurities are not of God. There are numerous people who are fulfilled with joy and happiness and are living a righteous life. They're living and breathing the life that is pleasing to God. As you probably already know, Sasha has returned and is still with the Savior. If you don't mind, recite with me in Psalm 23:4, "Yea though I walk through the valley of the shadow of death I will fear no evil for thou art with me; thy rod and thy staff they comfort me." For someone who has been through it, although I placed myself into many predicaments, I can still help in assisting others not to follow in my footsteps. Can I converse to you?

Our Father, the creator of the heaven as well as the earth, He knows of the things to come. So when we walk to and through the valley of our troubles, it is quite natural to trust in God. When he leads us through a path, He teaches and strengthens us causing to feel humble, faithful, and knowing that God is in control. If I could really see in the midst of my darkness, my valley, I would have called on God before I got deeper and deeper into trouble.

Growing up, my mother dragged me to church every Sunday until I was able to go to church without kicking and screaming. I was involved in the church choir and attending Bible study. My mother and I were joined at the hips. It was then that her financial struggles gave me enough ammunition to lose my faith. I thought, *How can God do this to a faithful woman?* It was then that I began to resent God. Even though my mother kept her faith, I couldn't. My mother would say, "God blessed me with a home and the ability to pay every dime of my mortgage bill with money to spare. I may not be able to do much else, but I'm blessed." She worked hard to make ends meet, and I wondered how could a faithful woman work two jobs after my father was injured on his job and was no longer able to work? They struggled so hard to rub two nickels together. Why couldn't God intervene? My higher education in any university was compromised because of money. Community college was on the menu, but I was only able to order one year. My resentment for God rested in my heart and in my soul until God handled me in another way. *I couldn't see what she was seeing.* "Praise God," she would say. But for what? I complained for all of us. I didn't get it, or should I say, I didn't understand her journey she had with God until now. Her faith kept her in peace with God and herself; she trusted Him with everything. I didn't know this before, but when she retired in her early years in life, she traveled the world with my father. God showed her favor at her workplace in providing her with a better income but most of all with one job. When my father passed on, my mother continued to live her life until God claimed her soul.

Let Sasha tell you more about Christ that she wasn't able to tell before. I can forewarn you about the enemy that I wasn't able to do beforehand. Let Sasha tell you that Satan presents himself in many ways. In where he doesn't succeed, he'll try, try, and try again. He will exhaust himself until he becomes successful or may accept his failure. A persistent devil, isn't he? It is imperative to know how not to become a victim of Satan and become acquainted with the Word of God. Establish a relationship with Him to build a strong foundation. My weakness was yearning to live in a high society, and Satan knew exactly what he needed to do in order to use it to his advantage.

"Yea, though walk through the valley of the shadow of death," the territory of darkness where Satan roams to imprison his prey. Flesh to bones is his home décor of the lost spirits who haven't made it through the valley. I have roamed in the valley and didn't need any assistance in finding any directions because I didn't know that I was in the valley. Everything was fine when I met someone who was qualified to carry out my needs and desires. I was a lost sheep who found every way to separate from the Shepherd. Christ the Shepherd looks after His flock; God who guides His people with care. I was glad to finally discover that "the Lord is my light and my salvation; who shall I fear? The Lord is the strength of my life; of who shall I be afraid" (Psalms 27:1). When I was conscious to the fact that God is my light, I was also conscious of the fact that I was walking in the valley where darkness encircled me coldheartedly. I was walking in the valley where the path was not of God. Satan ruled this path. This path was cold. Instead of falling on my knees and calling on God, I placed on my coat for warmth. The path was wet and stormy on occasion, and yet my foolishness overclouded my judgment and used an oversized umbrella for shelter. The path was hot with an unbearable heat wave, but I had a remedy for that as well. I placed the "top of the line" sunscreen and tried to stay in the shade as much as possible. This path had ditches and unstable foundation, but for this, I had to tread lightly and watch where I traveled from one point to the next. I had the answer for all things with the refusal in accepting Christ in my life. I didn't carry the faith that God can take care of me and my needs. My life was good, really good, but at times, I ran into some brick walls. With my daily requirements, I wasn't willing to sacrifice anything unto the Lord since I had everything I needed. What I didn't have, I made sure I obtained it. I was in darkness without a vision for life, but little did I know, God has always been there. Through the valley, the presence of God made my darkness into a shadow. His light illuminated my spirit with hope, and I knew what had to be done. The foundation was placed when my mother dragged me to church. Her faith strengthened her spirit and her soul, and it was time for me to stop compromising my standards and return to Christ. When breath still lingers in your body, it is not too late to surrender unto Christ. He is waiting, so what are you waiting for?

Related References:
Crown Financial Ministeries
www.crown.org

Greed:

> "Therefore consider the members of your earthly body as dead to ...greed, which amounts to idolatry" (Colossians 3:5).

> "He said to them, 'Beware, and be on your guard against every form of greed; for not even when one has an abundance does his life consist of his possessions'" (Luke 12:15).

> "Besides You, I desire nothing on earth" (Psalm 73:25).

> "The greedy man curses and spurns the Lord" (Psalm 10:3-4).

> "The treacherous will be caught by their own greed" (Proverbs 11:6).

Honesty:

> "The heart is more deceitful than all else and is desperately sick" (Jeremiah 17:9).

"It is the Spirit who bears witness, because the Spirit is the truth" (1 John 5:7).

"Keep your tongue from evil, and your lips from speaking deceit" (Psalm 34:13).

"A truthful witness saves lives, but he who speaks lies is treacherous" (Proverbs 14:25).

"Better is the poor who walks in his integrity, than he who is crooked though he be rich" (Proverbs 28:6).

Idolatry:

"You shall not make other gods besides Me; gods of silver or gods of gold, you shall not make for yourselves" (Exodus 20:23).

"Their idols are silver and gold, the work of man's hands" (Psalm 115:4).

"The idols of the nations are but silver and gold, the work of man's hands" (Psalm 135:15).

"All of her [Israel] idols will be smashed, all of her earnings will be burned with fire, and all of her images I [the Lord] will make desolate" (Micah 1:7).

"And you [God's people] will defile your graven images, overlaid with silver, and your molten images plated with gold. You will scatter them as an impure thing; and say to them, 'Be gone!' Then He will give you rain for the seed which you will sow in the ground, and bread from the yield of the ground, and it will be rich and plenteous; on that day your livestock will graze in a roomy pasture" (Isaiah 30:22-23).

Riches:

"He [the wicked man] will not become rich, nor will his wealth endure" (Job 15:29).

"Surely every man walks about as a phantom; surely they make an uproar for nothing; he amasses riches, and does not know who will gather them" (Psalm 39:6).

"Riches do not profit in the day of wrath, but righteousness delivers from death" (Proverbs 11:4).

"For what does it profit a man to gain the whole world, and forfeit his soul? For what shall a man give in exchange for his soul?" (Mark 8:36-37).

"Instruct those who are rich in this present world not to be conceited or to fix their hope on the uncertainty of riches, but on God" (1 Timothy 6:17).

Contentment:

"Let your character be free from the love of money, being content with what you have; for He Himself has said, 'I will never desert you, nor will I ever forsake you,' so that we confidently say, "The Lord is my helper, I will not be afraid" (Hebrews 13:5-6).

"If we have food and covering, with these we shall be content" (1 Timothy 6:8).

"Besides You, I desire nothing on earth" (Psalm 73:25).

"But godliness actually is a means of great gain, when accompanied by contentment" (1 Timothy 6:6).

Counsel:

"A wise man will hear and increase in learning, and a man of understanding will acquire wise counsel" (Proverbs 1:5).

"The way of a fool is right in his own eyes, but a wise man is he who listens to counsel" (Proverbs 12:15).

"O great and mighty God. The Lord of hosts is His name; great in counsel and mighty in deed" (Jeremiah 32:18-19).

"He who walks with wise men will be wise" (Proverbs 13:20).

"For to one is given the word of wisdom through the Spirit" (1 Corinthians 12:8).

Coveting:

"You shall not covet you neighbor's house; you shall not covet your neighbor's wife or his male servant or his female servant or his ox or his donkey or anything that belongs to your neighbor" (Exodus 20:17).

"You shall not covet your neighbor's wife, and you shall not desire your neighbor's house, his field or his male servant or his female servant, his ox or his donkey or anything that belongs to your neighbor" (Deuteronomy 5:21).

"You shall not covet the silver or the gold that is on them [graven images], nor take it for yourselves, lest you be snared by it, for it is an abomination to the Lord your God" (Deuteronomy 7:25).

"Now these things [Lord's discipline of Israel] happened as examples for us, that we should not crave evil things, as they also craved" (1 Corinthians 10:6).

"Do not be deceived; neither fornicators... nor the covetous... shall inherit the kingdom of God" (1 Corinthians 6:9-10).

Debt:

"The rich rules over the poor, and the borrower becomes the lender's slave" (Proverbs 22:7).

"Let the creditor seize all that he [the wicked] has; and let strangers plunder the product of his hand" (Psalm 109:11).

"Thus says the Lord... 'To whom of My creditors did I sell you? Behold, you were sold for your iniquities'" (Isaiah 50:1).

"The wicked borrows and does not pay back, but the righteous is gracious and gives" (Psalm 37:21).

CPSIA information can be obtained at www.ICGtesting.com
Printed in the USA
BVOW06s0223020816

457641BV00025B/157/P